BLEED LIKE ME

Also by C. Desir

Fault Line

BLEED LIKE ME

C. DESIR

Simon Pulse

New York   London   Toronto   Sydney   New Delhi

SIMON PULSE

An imprint of Simon & Schuster Children's Publishing Division

1230 Avenue of the Americas, New York, NY 10020

First Simon Pulse hardcover edition October 2014

Text copyright © 2014 by Christa Desir

Jacket photograph copyright © 2014 by Getty Images

For information about special discounts for bulk purchases, please contact Simon & Schuster Special Sales at 1-866-506-1949 or business@simonandschuster.com.

The Simon & Schuster Speakers Bureau can bring authors to your live event. For more information or to book an event contact the Simon & Schuster Speakers Bureau at 1-866-248-3049 or visit our website at www.simonspeakers.com.

Jacket designed by Jessica Handelman

Interior designed by Ellice M. Lee

The text of this book was set in New Caledonia.

Manufactured in the United States of America

2 4 6 8 10 9 7 5 3

Library of Congress Cataloging-in-Publication Data

Desir, Christa.

Bleed like me / Christa Desir. — First Simon Pulse hardcover edition.

p. cm.

Summary: Two emotionally scarred teenagers enter into a passionate, dangerous romance.

[1. Emotional problems—Fiction. 2. Love—Fiction.] I. Title.

PZ7.D4506Bl 2014

[Fic]—dc23

2013031611

ISBN 978-1-4424-9890-7 (hc)

ISBN 978-1-4424-9894-5 (eBook)

To all my tethers. Thank you for keeping me grounded.

I would be lost without you.

Acknowledgments

This book exists because agent Sarah LaPolla asked for a YA *Sid and Nancy* on Twitter. Twenty minutes later I sent an idea to her, and five minutes after that she replied with "Yes. Do this. I was hoping *you* would take up the challenge." I will forever be grateful for all of Sarah's enthusiasm, support, and ideas for making *Bleed Like Me* the best book it could be.

Equally immense gratitude goes to the formidable and fearless Liesa Abrams, who understands me in a way that few people do. It is an amazing thing to have an editor who takes risks and pushes you to be the best author you can be. It is an even more amazing thing to have an editor whose brain clicks with yours in such a way that neither of you turns away from the hard stuff. Liesa, thank you for your big ideas and your unflinching willingness to take on this book and the package of me.

To my dear friend and critique partner Lucy, I don't think I could've ever found Brooks inside of me if you hadn't introduced me to your Joseph first. There are no words for your brilliance. To Jolene and Jay and Carrie, thanks for existing. Thanks for sticking with me in spite of myself. And to Ellen Hopkins, who has fought for my books fiercely and has been a great mentor. You all make it easier for me to breathe in this writing world.

To all the people at Simon Pulse, thank you for making my life manageable. Michael Strother, I cannot tell you how much I rely on your wisdom and your energy. Patrick Price and Bethany Buck, you are absolutely my two favorite "handlers." I would sit next to you at any party and try desperately not to be awkward. A huge thank-you to the art, publicity, marketing, and education and library teams at Simon & Schuster. You are all incredible.

To Jonathan Lyons at Curtis Brown, Ltd. You are a super-stealthy agent with a heck of a work ethic, and for this I am immensely grateful. You also have a huge brain and amazing legal chops, and you don't seem to mind all my crazy. You and I are funny together and we fit, which I quite like; thanks for being one of my J's.

To all of my dear writer friends and teens who beta read and critiqued this book. It takes a village to make a novel, and all of you brought so much to this party. Katy, Alexis, Kari, Brooke, Jena, Rida, Derek, Amy, Carrie (who has been with me since the very beginning), and all my other bloggy friends, a world of gratitude for all of you. To SCBWI and the incredible writing community at large, you make this one of the most fun jobs in the world. To the Fourteenery, who have more combined wisdom than any group I have ever met, thanks for *everything* . . . you are seriously the most spectacular writing collective I know, and I still can't believe you took me on.

To my real-life friends and family, I cannot say enough how much your support and forgiveness have meant to me. Writers sort of suck to be around when they're in the thick of things. We spend too much time in our heads, and our insecurity takes up most of the space in the room. I have no excuses for the times when I am subhuman. And you have forgiven me over and over again. I hope the longer it goes on, I will find better balance. In the meantime, thank you for your patience and grace. I am nothing without you.

And finally, to Julio and my kids. You four are the reason I keep going. You make me the best person I can be. You keep me grounded. You love me unconditionally, and you make waking up every morning awesome. Thank you for believing in me. Thank you for traveling with me on this journey. I can't wait for a lifetime of adventures with you. I love you all so much.

PART I

1

I wasn't supposed to be born. My mom's doctors had told her over and over that severe endometrial scarring would make it practically impossible for her to carry a baby. But my infant self didn't care about scarring. Or the partial hysterectomy Mom had to get after my delivery. And for most of my childhood, we were happy in our little pod of three—Mom, Dad, me. Until my parents got a different notion about the magic number three: adopting three boys from Guatemala.

And I learned to disappear.

It was easier for everyone. I became the quiet one. The one who didn't drain my parents of everything they had. Pathetic as it might sound, going to school and working at the Standard Hardware were the good things in my life. When I wasn't there, I was tucked away in my bedroom, coming out only to referee arguments between Mom and my brothers when one of the neighbors called about the noise. Or to help when Mom gave me the ragged, desperate face she had on now as I stood at the open front door. Her gray roots were an inch thick at the crown of her head, and she was wearing the same outfit she slipped on every day after work: stained, discolored T-shirt, saggy sweatpants with too-loose elastic at the waist.

"Luis has locked himself in the bathroom again and Alex won't eat any of his snack until Luis comes out." Her exhausted voice passed through me. I'd heard it for almost five years, too long to even remember what the Mom of my childhood sounded like.

I dropped my messenger bag at my feet and opened the drawer of the small side table next to the overloaded coatrack in the hall. I plucked one of the emergency hotel key cards from its box and took the stairs two at a time. My heavy boots squeaked on the scuffed hardwood. The loud explosions from Miguel's Call of Duty game echoed from the living room.

I pounded on the bathroom door at the top of the stairs. "Luis. Get out of there."

"Fuck off."

Jesus. What did the other fifth graders think of this kid? He spent more time in the guidance counselor's office than in his own classroom. But no amount of "be respectful and appropriate" lecturing from my parents or school officials made a dent in his colorful vocabulary.

I shimmied the card along the edge of the doorjamb, wiggling it into just the right spot. *Click.* I swung the door open. The bathroom was trashed. Toilet paper and shaving cream were everywhere. A bottle of cough syrup sat sideways on the sink, its contents spilled all over the toothpaste and toothbrushes. Not quite a childproof cap after all.

Luis stood with his arms crossed. Brown, unapologetic face, black eyes boring into me as if I were personally responsible for the crap state of his life. "That cunt won't let me play video games."

I squeezed my eyes shut. He'd trashed the bathroom over a video game? I shook my head. Mom didn't deserve this even if she did sign up for it. "Clean it up."

"Fuck off."

"Clean it up or I'll hide Alex's blankie."

His eyes flared in alarm and then burned in hatred. The kid didn't care one bit about himself, but threaten one of his brothers and he came out swinging. He snatched a washcloth from the drawer and dropped it onto the cough syrup mess. "I'm gonna get my brothers out of this shithole. Soon."

"I'm first," I mumbled.

"What?" he asked, pausing in his half-assed cleanup job. "What did you say?"

"Nothing."

I pointed to the washcloth and he started sopping up the mess again. His thin shoulders shook as he muttered curses. I called down the stairs to Mom, "He's out. Tell Alex he'll be there in five minutes."

"I need to go to the library to study," I said at dinner, pushing leftover spaghetti across my plastic plate.

Dinner was the worst time of the day. The "pretend we're a happy family" time where cell phones weren't allowed and we all had to announce two things we'd learned in school. Two. Things. Did my parents ever even go to high school?

Mom had become an expert in making every meal in under eighteen minutes. Eighteen minutes was the maximum allowable time she could leave the boys without chaos erupting. I had no idea how she'd figured this out statistically, but I trusted her on it and got used to dinners that came frozen in bags or popped out of the microwave. Family "together" time was loud boys barking orders at Mom.

My parents had adopted my brothers off the streets of Guatemala City when they were six, four, and three. They were only going to take one of them, but they could tell the brothers were bonded and they wanted to keep them as a unit. We'd had so many family discussions about the benefits of siblings. I was twelve then and just starting to get pissy about being the sole focus of my parents' relentless hovering. Mom stared at babies everywhere we went, then came home and gushed about how her sister had been her best friend growing up. The sister who'd moved to Germany and rarely called anymore. My dad said he'd always wanted brothers. They both promised it would change all our lives. It did, but not like any of us expected.

"I need to go to the library to study," I said again, between Luis's demands for more milk and Alex's complaints about how he got too many tomato chunks in his sauce.

"I need to go to the library to study." Repeating sentences three times gave me the best chance of them actually sinking in.

I hadn't been to the library since seventh grade. But I was testing out the ratio of success in getting away from my brothers. Good lies need to be tucked away for emergency use. Most people don't realize this and use them too frequently, so they're no longer effective. Big mistake.

"You can study here," Mom answered, the desperate "don't leave me with these monsters" look flashing across her face.

"It's too loud and—" Before I could finish, Luis snatched Miguel's dinner roll from his plate, and then Miguel punched him hard enough to make Luis squeal.

Cue sibling fistfight number three. A new record for family dinner.

I scraped my half-eaten spaghetti into the trash and ran upstairs while Mom pulled the boys apart. I glanced in the mirror: jeans, black T-shirt, hoodie, boots, stripy hair, chain necklaces, too-pale face, too-thin body. Still the same me. Sometimes I would squint when I looked in the mirror and imagine I was someone else living a different life, but the blur never lasted. The dinginess of my room and the hollowness of my eyes always broke the illusion.

My boots thunked on the stairs as I headed back down, grabbing my bag before returning to the kitchen. When I walked in, Mom was standing at the counter, dropping more dinner rolls onto a baking sheet and lecturing the boys about how they should just ask her to make more if they're still hungry.

"Okay, I'm going."

"Be back before ten." Mom waved at me and continued her lecture. Alex flashed his missing-tooth grin and then flipped me off as Mom turned away. Nice. Miguel and Luis were kicking each other under the kitchen table when I walked out. A crash followed by a shriek from Mom punctuated the door click behind me.

The skate park stayed open until eight on weeknights in September, closing for the season on October first. I walked to it on autopilot, having spent so many summer afternoons watching my brothers fly up and down the ramps. They bitched endlessly about the helmet requirement, but after two trips to the ER for stitches, they'd gotten the point about head injuries.

The night was cool and quiet. I parked myself on top of the high hill I normally sat on to watch the hard-core skaters practice. A chain-link fence surrounded the ramps, and on a clear night I could see the blinking lights of the Chicago skyline in the distance. I lit a menthol cigarette and blew rings of smoke toward the dusky sky. I shut my eyes and listened to the boards zipping down ramps and the low voices trash talking and laughing. Did my parents ever watch me at the skate park when I was younger? Before the boys and all the trouble? I couldn't remember.

"Skate girl, huh?" a voice broke into my cocoon, and I blinked the menthol buzz away. A tall, too-thin boy stood in front of me, smirking. A bright blue patch of hair dropped in front of his left eye, and a retro Sex Pistols shirt clung to his lanky frame.

"What?" I blinked again and shook my head.

He gave me a small smile and shrugged. His eyes traced over me, and it took everything I had not to cross my arms over my chest and move away.

"Why aren't you with the rest of the chain-smokers at the Punkin' Donuts?" he said. He took a step toward me, and I slid back so I could see him better. My eyes dropped to the aerosol can and paper bag he held.

"What are you doing with that?"

He sprayed the can into the bag and stuck his face into the fumes. His chest puffed out as he inhaled. I pressed my hand into the grass beneath me, plucking at the cool wetness. Wetness I could feel along the back of my jeans.

He coughed and dropped the bag to his side. "Livening up the evening."

I looked him over again. The rest of his hair was dark brown like his eyes. His jeans hung low on his hips, but not in the annoying way where they practically fall off. The bones of his shoulders jutted out from his shirt. He grinned at me, slightly dazed.

"Are you retarded?"

"Nope," he said, and the grin cocked up even higher on the side of his mouth not hidden by hair.

"You sure? No one huffs here. It's country."

"Country?" He shook the can again.

"Yeah, as in it's for idiots who can't find better drugs."

He chuckled, and I stared at the way his hair fell across his dark eyes and clear skin. No acne. How does this even happen to guys? He brushed his long fingers over his mouth, and I followed them as they fell back to his side. Hands have always been interesting to me, and his moved too gracefully in comparison to the rest of him. Like they didn't know they were on the end of a sloppy boy.

"Well," he said, dropping the can into the paper bag,

"huffing wouldn't be my first choice, but we're in the suburbs. Sometimes you gotta work with what you've got."

"We're like three El stops from Chicago. My grandmother could score drugs in this town."

He shrugged. "Maybe I like the fumes." I looked him over again. The thumb of his left hand hooked in his jean pocket while his other fingers drummed against the denim.

"Huh. My brothers huffed on the streets of Guatemala to keep from getting too hungry." Why'd I tell him that? Why was I even talking to him? Shit. Shit. Shit.

He took another half step toward me. "Yeah? Your brothers are from Guatemala?"

"Adopted."

"Obviously." He motioned to my pale face and blue eyes. Something was written on his palm. I squinted to see, but it was too blurred.

Enough. I stood up and grabbed my messenger bag. "Okay. Well, it was nice meeting you. I'm gonna go talk to some of the boarders."

"What's your name?" He reached out and fingered the hoops running up the side of my ear. I flinched and knocked his hand away. Goose bumps prickled along the back of my neck. It'd been too long since someone touched me.

I took a step around him. "Amelia Gannon. But no one calls me Amelia. It's just Gannon."

He pushed his hair off his face, and I saw a metal bar peeking from his eyebrow. "Gannon. Yeah, I like that."

"Glad you approve. I live to please. Really." I slid my pack of cigarettes into my pocket. I took a step to the side and he countered. People normally weren't this interested in having a conversation with me. I crossed my leg behind me and stared at him for an uncomfortable amount of time. "So?"

His eyes looked glazed, and it occurred to me his interest might be more from the fume high than anything else. It made sense. I wasn't exactly the kind of girl guys got in big conversations with, even random blue-haired boys with eyebrow piercings and nice hands.

"So what?" he said, reaching out to trace my hoops again.

"Dude, back off." I grabbed his wrist and dug my nails in. "Why are you touching me?"

He dropped his hand. "I like your hoops. They're sexy."

My cheeks heated, but I squinted my eyes at him. "Listen, whatever your name is, you can't just go around touching people. You'll get your ass handed to you."

He tilted his head back and laughed. His Adam's apple bobbed along his slender neck. I gulped as something warm pooled in my stomach. Shit.

"What are you doing here?" I asked. "Are you a boarder?"

He snorted. "Fuck, no. I was never sober enough to learn

when everyone else was figuring it out. Seems kind of stupid to try it now."

"You mean when everyone learned in, like, fifth grade? One of those child addicts, eh?"

His face froze for a half second, but then he grinned. "Something like that." He drummed his fingers on his jeans again. "So do you skate?"

"No. Not in a long time. Too busy working. I just come here for the amusement of watching guys fall on their asses."

He grinned. "One of those types, then?"

"What types?"

He looked me up and down, and my stomach knotted. "The angry girls."

My fingers tightened around the strap of my bag. "Not quite."

He leaned closer. "Then what type are you?"

"I'm not any type." I inched back. My strong instinct to bolt warred with the depressing realization that I had no place to go and the even sadder fact that this guy was the first guy in a long time to talk to me without asking for money or cigarettes.

"So where do you work?" he said, dropping to the grass and patting the spot next to him.

I didn't move. "Standard Hardware."

He patted the spot again. I stared at his fingers and tilted my head, trying to decide if he was being friendly or stalky. Chitchat wasn't my strong suit, so it was hard to say. He released a sigh before yanking me next to him. I scrambled to get up, but then his hand touched my side and I froze.

"Relax, Gannon. It's a nice night. I want to talk to you. You don't have to be so cagey."

I shifted away and narrowed my eyes. He offered me a goofy boy grin. I hugged my knees to my chest and focused on the boarders.

He grunted. "So a job at the hardware store must mean you know your way around tools?"

I couldn't help smiling. "Yeah. Pretty much."

His hands moved to the sleeve of my hoodie and he brushed away a piece of dried grass. His fingers lingered over the outside of my wrist before I snatched my hand away.

"I like girls who know their way around tools."

"Are you being gross?"

He laughed and nudged me with his elbow. "That's *your* head in the gutter, not mine."

"What did you say your name was?"

"Michael Brooks. But Brooks to you. Okay?"

I shrugged.

"So . . ."—he picked at a piece of loose string on the edge of my jeans—"do you want to hang out for a while?"

"Not really." I had nowhere to go, but I still wasn't sure

about Mr. Grabby Hands Brooks. Or my weird response to him.

He chuckled. "You don't like me?"

"You're a little handsy for my taste."

He laughed harder and pulled his hand back from the loose string. "Not normally. It must be something about you."

It was a line. It had to be. But why was I being singled out to be on the receiving end of cheesy lines? "What are you talking about? You just met me."

"I go to your school."

I stretched my legs out in front of me. "Since when?"

"Three weeks ago. Haven't you seen me?"

I turned to him and laughed in his face. "It's a big school. And why would I have noticed you?"

"I've seen you," he said, and shifted his knee so it touched mine. The warmth of his leg made me feel strange and, if I was being completely honest, a little bit good. "Come on. Let me walk you home."

"You're not walking me home. I'm not telling you where I live."

"Okay, I'll walk you somewhere else, then."

"Who even said I was leaving?"

He nodded to the flickering street lamp behind us. "Skate park's closing soon. What're your plans for the rest of the evening? Is there any place else you'd like to watch guys fall on their asses?"

I pulled my phone out of my messenger bag to check the time. It was too early to consider going home. My brothers would still be up.

"I think I'll stay here a little while longer."

He inched close enough that his whole thigh pressed fully against mine. "Me too, then."

I shrugged and tamped down the heat on my cheeks, grateful for the growing darkness. "Suit yourself." I held out my pack of cigarettes. "Want one?"

He scoffed. "Filtered menthols? I don't think so. I smoke real cigarettes."

I lit another cigarette and dropped my lighter into my pocket. Smoke curled around me, and wetness from the ground seeped further into the back of my pants. But the warmth of Brooks's too-close leg kept me from paying much attention to the cold discomfort. Neither of us said a word. I opened my mouth to ask what he was doing there in the first place, but somehow the question felt like an intrusion into the strange peace blanketing the night.

2

I'd gotten a job at Standard because it was a really good way to avoid my family on the weekends. My boss, Dennis, liked me and let me fiddle with all the tools and even showed me how to use most of them. When I wasn't scheduled to work, I planted myself in the storage garage across the alley behind the store. Graffiti riddled the outside of the garage, but no one had managed to break into it. Dennis had two industrial-strength padlocks on the outside and had only given me a key to them after I'd been working at Standard a full year. And even then it was because he'd gotten sick one day and I'd had to track him down at his compulsively tidy bachelor-pad apartment to open everything up.

The best part of the storage garage was all the stuff I could build out of scrap or slightly deformed wood. It wasn't rocket science, but it took a certain kind of concentration to work a circular saw and that made everything else in my brain shut off.

Carpentry can be both an art and a science. On top of me not having the best quality wood, things occasionally got mucked up. Especially when I was impatient or doing half-baked rush jobs. I'd learned how to make some cool things out of screwed-up projects or even how to change the design of a project to fit in with my mistakes. There were tools for almost everything, and over the past two years I'd fiddled with almost all of them.

My hands moved automatically over pieces of wood, plucking one that appeared to be the right size. I marked lengths with measuring tape and drew cut lines using my T square. My movements were quick, focused, confident.

I'd been working on a low bookshelf for my room. Nothing too elaborate, but a place to keep my movies. Yeah, I collected movies when everyone and their brother streamed. I liked vintage. I got DVDs at garage sales for a dollar and had a collection of almost a hundred.

The shelves had been the trickiest part because I'd beveled the edges so the movies could sit on a slant. I'd gone through my entire vocabulary of swears and an embarrassing amount of wood before I finally got them how I wanted.

Now I was making a small door to attach to the front of the shelf. No sense tempting my brothers with the sight of my movies. Not that a closed door wasn't temptation enough.

"Gannon."

I looked up from the belt sander to see Ali with her hands on her hips, tapping the toe of her Converse, her bleached hair pulled into three random topknots. I flicked the power button off the sander and raised the safety goggles Dennis made me wear.

"What?"

"How long are you gonna be here?"

Ali was my best friend, but we both had enough shit going on in our lives to use the term loosely. I suspected Ali was as paranoid of people getting in her business as I was. She lived with her mom and on most nights, her mom's skeevy boyfriend, Dave. I'd only met the douche bag once, but his gaze hadn't left the curve of Ali's ass one time during our conversation. Classy.

"I'm almost done. What do you need?"

"Fortification."

This was my and Ali's code for bumming cigarettes off each other. She was the only other girl I knew who smoked filtered menthols, and if either one of us was without, we could pretty much count on the other. Though nine out of ten times I was Ali's supplier. Her mom wouldn't let her work because her grades sucked, so she spent most of her time hanging out at the Punkin' Donuts across the street from Standard, bumming cigarettes off other people until they tired of her.

"Well's dry at the Punkin', huh?"

"Yeah. Plus, no menthol smokers today."

I put away the sander and rubbed sawdust onto the thighs of my jeans. I tossed the goggles into a pile in the corner of the garage and grabbed my bag before locking up.

"Dennis," I shouted, walking through the back door of the store, a tiny alarm beep signaling my entrance.

"Yes?" A shock of white hair popped out from the plumbing-supply aisle. Dennis's dorky red vest tugged across the pooch of his stomach. His glasses were carefully taped on one side, and his plaid shirt was tucked into his jeans.

"Ali and I are taking a break. I'll be back in ten minutes. I locked the garage, but I'm not done in there."

He nodded at Ali and turned his wrinkled face to me. "Don't light up in front of the store. My customers keep complaining about the smoke."

I frowned. "Okay."

"And don't be gone too long. I'm gonna clock you in to help me with this paint-sample display when you get back."

I slung my messenger bag over my shoulder. "You could have called Ricardo," I said. "I'm not even supposed to be here today."

Ricardo was Dennis's other high school employee. He was really mellow and didn't mind the crap jobs around the store. I covered his shifts when he had soccer games, and in exchange he cleaned the bathroom without complaining.

"Ricardo doesn't like me as much as you," Dennis said. I snorted. Ricardo was the most agreeable kid I'd ever met. He willingly put up with hours of bullshit monthly window-display adjustments, while I bailed after twenty minutes of Dennis's fussing. "Also, he had a game, and since it was just a small endcap display, I figured you could handle it. You're here anyways."

I shook my head. "What're you going to do when I graduate and quit?"

Dennis laughed. "You won't quit. You like me too much. You and Ricardo will be here forever." He said this all the time, and I vacillated between accepting his words as the truth and wanting to vomit at the idea of being stuck in the same town forever. As it was, I squirreled away the money I didn't spend on cigarettes in hopes of one day getting out of Dodge.

Since Dennis only had the store, he treated Ricardo and me like we were his kids or something. And even though Ricardo was way more willing to put up with stuff, I suspected I was Dennis's favorite. His messed-up, chain-smoking, surly favorite.

"I'll be starting a 401(k) for you soon," Dennis continued as I waved and pointed Ali toward the door. "Then I bet you'll want some sort of company car. And probably health insurance." He patted his stomach like a sadistic Santa.

I shook my head and snatched a candy bar from a large box next to the front exit.

"You'll have to pay for that. It's not part of your company benefits," Dennis called.

"Okay. Dock it from my paycheck." It was an ongoing joke between us. Since I'd started working at Standard, no one had ever bought candy from the shop. Dennis threw away tons of it every six months but still insisted on buying more to display in a large dusty box in front. I secretly suspected he kept buying it for snacks for the three of us.

My steps fell in line with Ali's as we moved past the front window and down the street. Loud music blared from one of the cars passing by us. Ali did a little spin dance move and nudged me.

"Have you seen the new kid with the blue hair?" she asked. Her shoes squeaked as she walked, and I eyed the fishnet-Converse combo she sported.

"You should wear boots with fishnets."

She turned and dropped her eyes to my ratty jeans, too-small hoodie, and clunky work boots. "You're giving me fashion advice now?"

Yeah. Ali and I weren't really girlfriends that way. "Just saying."

She crossed her arms. "So have you seen him?"

I reached up to touch the hoops on my ear. "Not really."

Ali arched a pierced brow at me. "Not really? What does that mean? Have you seen him or not?"

I shrugged and she rolled her eyes. Lack of verbal commitment worked for me. I shared cigarettes, not gossip. Plus, I wasn't sure what to say. *We hung out, sort of. We mostly sat. I smoked. He laughed at the skaters. And bumped knees with me a few too many times for it to be an accident. But I have no idea what he wants with me.*

We walked beneath the El bridge and I shivered in the cool autumn air. My hoodie had been washed too many times and had lost most of its warmth. Getting a new one involved either busting into my work funds, asking Mom to take me shopping, or asking her to pick one up for me. All options with an equal lack of appeal. Easier to just be cold.

The minute we emerged from the shadow of the bridge back into the sun, I pulled my cigarettes out of my bag. Ali pulled one from the box and placed it between her dark-lined lips. She cupped her hands around my lighter and then took a long drag.

I slipped my lighter into my back pocket. "Do you still have Saturday detention?"

Ali played with the ring in her eyebrow and I swatted at her hand. "What?"

"It'll get infected."

Her fingers dropped to the bottom edge of one of the three T-shirts she wore. "Yep, Saturday detention, nine o'clock."

I never got why Ali always pushed to get Saturday detention until she told me one day at school that her mom got drunk on

Friday nights and almost always slept most of Saturday. The thought of her having to hang out with Skeevy Dave all day, waiting for her mom to get out of bed, made me want to throw up in my mouth.

"How many more weeks do you have on this one?"

She flicked an ash. "Three. Then I have to come up with something new."

Ali was obsessed with finding just the right thing to earn her Saturday detention without completely screwing up her chances of getting into state college. Most of our conversations revolved around plotting the next scheme.

"Any ideas?"

She pulled another drag from her cigarette and stubbed it out. "I heard about this kid who phoned in a bomb threat, but I think the police might get involved in that one."

I nodded. Ali pointed to my bag and I fished out another cigarette for her. She was about the fastest smoker I'd ever seen. It cost me more money, but that was the price of not being a complete loner.

"So," she continued, "I was thinking about maybe flooding the guys' locker room. You know? Sneaking in and turning on all the sinks and showers during a game."

"Pretty good. Funny. Crazy. It'll cause enough damage to warrant more than an afternoon detention. Yeah, I think it'll work."

"How long do you think Dennis will need you today?"

I stubbed out the rest of my cigarette and pocketed the butt. "Probably a half hour or so."

"Wanna hang out?"

I shrugged. Ali flicked her cigarette at me.

"Gannon. It's a simple question. Do you want to hang out or don't you? Do you already have plans?"

I shook my head and swallowed the weird bubbly desire to see Brooks and his good hands. "No. We can hang out."

I don't have the first frickin' clue how we ended up in the woods at someone's three-kegger. I usually hated that shit. Not the drinking so much as all the small talk required to fill my cup. It was annoying, and after my freshman year I'd avoided parties like the plague.

But Ali had some guy she was into and wanted to find him. After forty-five minutes of her pouting and begging, I finally agreed to go with her. Chasing guys wasn't my thing, and it hadn't ever been our thing to bond over hotties, but her buzzy eyes made me think maybe she was really into this one. I slid into her mom's car, and we made the twenty-minute drive to the woods with nothing but overly loud music between us.

"I'll get our first drinks," Ali said, pushing her way into the large crowd circling the keg. I moved to the picnic tables and dropped onto one of the benches. A giant bonfire crackled nearby, and huge speakers blared from both sides of the clearing. I zipped my hoodie all the way up.

I picked at the flaking paint on the table. Bodies whirled and danced around me. I curled my hands into my sleeves. Too many people were around. Too many people oblivious to my existence. I never should have agreed to come. Coolness seeped into my skin through my clothes.

I pulled my phone from my pocket and called Mom, hoping she'd insist I come home immediately. No answer. Of course. I knew she was home but couldn't pick up. I left a message telling her I was with Ali and would be home late. I didn't give her a time. She'd be asleep anyway, her body drained from a too-long day of wrangling boys between the soccer games they'd probably gotten kicked out of and the therapy appointments they hated.

"I didn't take you for a party kind of girl." Brooks's voice wrapped around me like a scarf, and something inside my stomach flipped.

"I'm not. I'm doing a favor for a friend."

He sat on the bench, his thighs straddling it so his knees bumped against me. "Which friend?"

He pushed my hair back and teased his fingers over the hoops in my ear. I smacked his hand and pointed to Ali. She had her tongue in some guy's mouth and had dropped the cups she was holding to wrap her arms around his neck. Great.

"She seems to be doing okay on her own."

I nodded. This was exactly why I never got involved with Ali and her boyfriend drama. I was always left trapped in some random place with no ride, waiting for her hookup to be over.

Brooks moved closer to me and pressed his knee along my thigh. "Let me guess. That's your ride?"

I nodded, unwilling to let him hear a hitch in my voice.

He popped up. "It's your lucky day, then. Come on." He held his hand out to me.

"Are you taking me home?"

"No. For a walk."

I crossed my arms. "Dude. I'm not taking a walk in the woods with you. I've seen that movie and have no interest in starring in it. I'll wait for Ali."

He gripped my hips and hauled me up. Huh. Stronger than I'd guessed. He unzipped my hoodie and his cold fingers pushed the neck of my shirt to the side. I should stop this. But I was frozen to my spot. His thumb dipped into the hollow skin near my collarbone. "Don't cover this up."

I blinked twice. "What? Why?"

"Because it may be my favorite part of you."

I batted his hand away. "Have you been drinking?"

"Maybe. But the better question is, why aren't you?"

"I don't answer questions."

He grinned and my stomach flipped again. "Of course you don't. Now come with me."

"Why?"

He leaned forward and I thought he might kiss me. Here. In front of everyone. My fingers curled into a fist, ready to coldcock him. But his lips found my ear instead. "Because I know you really want to. Come on. You aren't talking to anyone. You don't have to sit here alone."

Then his hand was on my back, guiding me away. I didn't even wave good-bye to Ali. Just followed the press of his hand and the sound of his boots crunching along the path through the woods. He hummed a little, and I watched him through the veil of blue hair covering his eyes.

We hadn't gone more than twenty feet into the woods when a loud voice called out.

"Brooks. We're going swimming. You coming?"

Four obviously drunk guys stood by the clearing to the river, pulling their shirts off.

My eyes widened and I turned to Brooks. "It's not even fifty degrees out. You can't be serious."

He grinned and pushed the blue hair from his face. "Gannon. I might as well tell you now, there isn't much I say no to."

My heart thunked at the weird declaration.

"You'll freeze."

"Are you worried?" He tucked me under his arm, and I

relaxed into his warmth for a second before elbowing him.

"I'm not worried. I just think you're psychotic."

"Brooks. Are you coming?" one of the guys bellowed again. They had peeled off their jeans and stood waiting like overly steroided plucked chickens.

"Give me a second," Brooks called back. The guys grumbled, but then turned and sprinted to the river. Several seconds of screaming and "Holy shit, it's frickin' cold" followed.

Brooks pulled me against a tree. "You should come with me."

"Hell, no. I don't do hypothermia."

He started to tug at the bottom of my shirt, and I dug my fingernails into his arm until he let go.

"It'll be fun." He leaned in to me, and I bit my tongue to keep from asking him what he thought he was doing. It was obvious. I just couldn't really believe it. Didn't know if I wanted to.

"I don't want people to see me." My eyes dropped. It was a stupid admission. Something I'd never offer to anyone else. The nearness of him was clouding my judgment. He was so close I felt a nipple ring through his thin shirt.

His mouth moved to mine, and he placed the tiniest kiss next to my bottom lip, then on my cheeks, forehead, along my jaw. *Yes. No. Crap.* I wanted him to press forward, but he pulled back instead. "Okay. Wait for me."

He stepped back and had his shirt off before I could move.

He turned, sliding his jeans down over his thin, muscular legs and kicking his shoes off, leaving him in nothing but a pair of plaid boxers. My breath caught when I saw the pale smooth marks on his back. I took a step forward and reached my hand out. He whipped around and squinted at me.

"Don't touch."

"What?" Even with the bonfire I wasn't sure what I was seeing. Were those scars? What the hell had happened to him?

"We'll talk about it later."

His finger traced my collarbone before he dropped another small kiss on my lips and then bolted for the water. His entire body submerged beneath the surface, and I waited for him to pop back up. Twenty seconds passed. My heart beat too fast and I started to get the overwhelming feeling that made my skin itch.

He came up laughing. I slid to the ground and hugged my knees, watching as he goaded the other guys into going under. The pale skin of his chest seemed to shine in the darkness. He looked over at me and grinned, shaking the wet hair out of his eyes like a puppy dog. He turned around, and I swallowed when I saw his back again. Scars from being whipped, maybe. My hands dropped to my lap, nails digging into my palms over and over. *Don't let him draw you in.*

3

Dennis made me haul paint cans into the storage garage for most of my shift the next day. It was exhausting, and I cursed him every time I saw him. He chuckled and offered to let me clean the bathroom instead. Ricardo, in his soccer jersey, Standard vest, and too-clean jeans, smirked and pointed to the toilet brush. I gave him the finger.

"Mop's lighter than a paint can," he teased.

"Yes, but walking into the bathroom is like bathing in a urinal. I won't even use it to wash my hands."

Ricardo laughed. "Yeah, I know. You sneak to the Punkin' and smoke, then use theirs. That bathroom is equally disgusting."

I shook my head. "No. It's not, because it's not unisex, so I don't fall in the toilet when some guy forgets to put the lid down or slip in a puddle of piss because none of you can aim to save your lives."

"Girls are just as disgusting. You wouldn't believe the crap I find in the trash."

I offered a widemouthed grin. "Which is exactly why I won't clean the bathroom."

Ricardo stared at the ceiling, his equivalent of the Ali eye roll, then pointed to the pile of paint cans. "Have fun, then."

By the time I was finished with all of them, my body ached so much I pulled a tarp into the corner of the garage and fell asleep. When I woke, I noticed Dennis had covered me with a sleeping bag and left my paycheck next to a cup of coffee. I gulped down the coffee and double-checked the padlocks on the garage before starting my nightly round of avoiding home.

The house was quiet by the time I stumbled in. It was after eleven, and my throat was raw from too many cigarettes. All three of my brothers were passed out in their large, messy room in a pile of arms and legs and ADD-inspired exhaustion. My parents had given them the biggest bedroom when it became clear they wouldn't sleep without one another. Mom and Dad had joined two smaller bedrooms for themselves and given me the back office to turn into my room. I went to the bathroom and heard my parents' voices through the thin walls.

"You baby them too much," Dad said. His voice had a sneering, critical edge that tunneled through me.

"They're just boys," Mom murmured, tired and pleading.

"They're old enough to do some of the bedtime routine on their own," he grumbled.

"They had to do that enough in Guatemala. We need to show them we'll always take care of them."

"You shouldn't be picking out their clothes and helping them get dressed. They're far too old for that. Luis in particular."

"He's only in fifth grade," she whispered.

"He's too old. Are you going to clean up after him when he has his first wet dream?"

The venom in Dad's voice made me jerk back.

"Go to hell, Richard. Don't put your insecurity on me." Mom's weak voice was laced with anger.

I covered my ears with my hands. Their words blended into white noise, and I breathed in and out of my mouth. I sat on the toilet, waiting until the angry muffles stopped. My brothers. It was always about my brothers. Or at least it had been since they came home with my parents. That'd been five years ago. Five years of therapy, five years of attachment issues, five years of shrieking. My skin itched everywhere.

I popped my head into the hallway and saw the light to my parents' room flick off. My shoulders dropped and I moved back toward the bathroom mirror. I stared at the dark circles beneath my eyes. I'd lost too much weight and looked shitty, even for me. I pushed my bleached bangs out of my face so they blended with the black and red streaks in the rest of my hair. Luis called me the freaky zebra girl. My makeup had started to streak on my face, but I was too exhausted to bother with taking it off. I gulped down a glass of water and crept back to my room.

The tiny light in the corner illuminated shadows across the dark chocolate walls. Horror-movie posters covered most of them. Tools peeked from a gray metal box in the corner. My banged-up laptop sat open on the small wooden desk I'd built from scrap lumber. I launched the Internet and reviewed the history. Porn sites. Luis. Stupid kid didn't even know how to erase where he'd been trolling. Evidently the wet dream was going to happen sooner rather than later.

My parents' words pinged around my head and I started to tremble. I flattened myself facedown on the worn-out quilt Mom had sewn for me when I was born, before she gave up sewing to patch together boys instead. I slid my hand under my bed, groping for the familiar plastic case tucked between my mattress and bed frame. My fingers brushed over it and something inside me uncoiled. I tugged out the polka-dot plastic makeup kit and unzipped it, my fingers shaking in anticipation. They moved over the razor blades and I got the dizzy, light-headed feeling I always got when I thought about cutting. I scratched off old blood from one of the razors with my nail.

I dropped my clothes into a pile on the floor and pulled on a large Cassius Clay T-shirt to sleep in. The material slid over my itchy skin, causing prickles along the back of my neck. I lifted the left side of the shirt and rubbed a circle in my flesh, spreading the skin above my hipbone. My stomach was the safest place to cut. My parents hated half shirts and bikinis, so there was no danger of anyone seeing scabs or scars. The razor slipped along the edge of my skin like a cat scratch. I pushed harder, the first tiny drops of blood popping out. It stung, and my breath came out with a whoosh. I retraced the line, harder the second time across. My skin, the razor, my blood, back and forth. The pain pierced me, poured over me. And finally, finally, I could breathe again.

Drip. Cut. Drip. Cut.

My parents' conversation, the anger in Mom's voice, the accusation in Dad's, all of it slipped away. There was only the point of the blade and the precision of knowing how not to go too deep. One. Two. Three cuts along the side of my stomach. Parallel and beautiful in their own way.

Cool air hit my exposed leg and my head jerked up. Brooks was sitting with his elbows on the ledge of my window, watching me. Oh God. Crap. The screen was open halfway and the window was pushed all the way up. Stupid brothers and their stupid water-balloon launching pad on the roof outside my room. I wanted to kill them.

Brooks's eyes drifted between the razor in my hand and the bloody scratches on my stomach. I dropped the razor into its case, dragged my shirt down, and slid to the floor, tucking the kit beneath the bed.

"What're you doing here?" I said, trying to blink away the post-cut euphoria.

His feet swung to the floor and he pulled himself inside. "You cut?"

"What're you doing here?" I whispered again. "What're you doing in my bedroom?"

"Visiting."

"Get out." I stood up and pointed to the window.

He pushed the screen down. "No. I told you, I'm just visiting."

"I didn't invite you."

He smiled. "Semantics. You did say 'I'll see you later' at the party when you took off. That's practically an invitation."

"'See you later' doesn't mean 'come stalk me at my house,' you freak."

He tucked his hands into his jean pockets and eyed my room. "So you like horror movies, huh?"

I glanced at the *Friday the 13th* and *Nightmare on Elm Street* posters on my walls and smiled a little. "Mostly eighties horror movies. Those are the really great ones. When they used fake blood and bad effects. Not the perfect CGI stuff they do today."

He mirrored my grin. "Have you seen *Happy Birthday to Me*?"

I gaped at him. "Of course. Have you?"

"Yep. What about *Sleepaway Camp*?"

I nodded and took a step closer to him. I'd never met anyone who'd seen *Sleepaway Camp*. "How have you seen those?"

"My mom had a collection of them. I watched them when I was bored and left to fend for myself," he said. "It was a pretty great time for horror movies. I saw the remake of *Prom Night* and it totally sucked in comparison to the original. It's like trying to remake *Star Wars*. You kinda want all the cheesy effects and bad acting."

The breeze from the window hit my legs again and I suddenly remembered where we were.

"My parents will kill you if they find you here."

Brooks took three steps toward me and tugged at the bottom of my shirt.

I swatted at his cold hands. "Get the hell away from me."

He didn't release his grip. "I wanna see your stomach."

The air froze in the room, too still and stifling. "Back off. I don't know what you're talking about."

He gave me a tiny grin. "Gannon. Surely you're not gonna lie to me? I watched you for the last few minutes. I wanna see your cuts."

"No. Back off. It's none of your business."

His hand loosened and his other hand lifted my chin. "I'm making you my business."

The memory of his soft lips in the woods flashed through my mind. I hated that his words made me want him. I hated to think I was *that* girl. The one who lifted her shirt because of warm lips, good taste in movies, and a caveman sense of possession.

I crossed my arms. "Why? Do you think you're gonna fix me?"

He laughed too loud and I reached up to cover his mouth. His tongue thrust forward and he licked my palm. I pulled back, but not before his teeth nipped my fingers. Christ, this boy was messing with my head.

"Hell no, I'm not gonna fix you. Look at me. Do I seem at all qualified to fix anyone?"

My eyes skimmed over his ratty shirt, low-riding jeans, and blue hair. He barely seemed qualified to dress himself. "Good point. Seriously. What are you doing here? How'd you find me?"

He grinned and the metal bar on his brow lifted. "Not too many other Amelia Gannons in the school directory."

"You looked for me in the school directory?"

"Yeah." His hand moved to the edge of my T-shirt again. I slapped it away. "I thought you might be kinda into me. Most people don't like me, but you seem different from the other people at school."

I closed my eyes against the reality of him in my room. This couldn't be happening. No guy had been in my room. Ever. I didn't do relationships. People didn't see me that way. Most people didn't see me at all. My hands curled around the edge of my T-shirt as I shored up my defenses.

"So you just popped over to my house and climbed through the window? Did you think you were gonna get laid? I'm not exactly into that whole *Romeo and Juliet* balcony scene."

Brooks leaned forward, then snatched my hand and swung me next to him on the bed. I struggled, but his arms locked around me. My body stilled and I met his eyes. He shook his hair back.

"I didn't think I'd be lucky enough to get laid tonight. But I thought you'd consider me."

I eased out of his grip. "Consider you what? A psycho who breaks into my room at eleven o'clock at night?"

"No," he said, letting me go and tracing the hoops along my ear. "Consider me your guy."

I rolled over and got to my feet. "Brooks. I'm not sure how to respond to that. I met you less than a week ago. This is kind of coming out of left field, you know?"

He sat on the edge of my bed and tapped a tune on his knees with his long, distracting fingers. "Yeah. But I still think you'll consider me."

I didn't say anything. The whole conversation was surreal,

even for my world. Brooks hopped up and moved toward the window. After two steps he turned back and snatched my razor case from under my bed. "You should give this shit up. I don't want you doing it anymore. We're not going to roll that way."

I snatched the case from his hands and held it behind my back. "We're not going to roll *any* way."

Brooks leaned toward me and dropped his mouth onto my neck. I slugged him, but he chuckled, and his warm tongue circled the spot above my collarbone until my knees almost gave out. Then he sucked my skin so hard I squeaked. He released me and swiveled us toward the long mirror in the corner of my room. His arm snaked around me, and his free hand tilted my head to the side to show me the hickey he'd just given me.

"No more cutting," he whispered. "I want to know about every mark that's on your body."

He released me and dropped out of my window so fast I couldn't even respond. I wanted to tell him to go to hell. I wanted to tell him to find someone else. I wanted to tell him I wasn't buying the shit he was selling. But I couldn't turn away from the mirror and the hideously beautiful mark on my neck.

Ali and I sat smoking on a parking bumper in front of the Punkin' Donuts the next day. Work was slow and Ricardo had offered to stay late so I could take off.

"So Skeevy Dave offered to get us Green Day tickets if we want."

I snorted. "Green Day? For real?"

Ali blew a long stream of smoke above my head. Her new tongue piercing flashed as she took another drag. "Don't be such a snob. I heard they're amazing in concert."

I shrugged and fiddled with the laces on my boots. "What's the catch?"

Ali tapped her feet. "Dave wants to come with us."

Ick. Gross. A thousand yucks. "And you're considering it?"

"Maybe. It *is* Green Day."

I put out my cigarette and looked at Ali. "And it *is* Skeevy Dave."

Ali blinked her overly charcoaled eyes at me before nodding. "Yeah, you're right. It's not worth it. I just thought it might be fun for a bunch of us to go."

Did a bunch of us include her boy toy from the woods? Part of me wanted to ask, but then I bit my tongue and pulled out another cigarette. Getting into that conversation with Ali would open a whole can of worms between us: an over-sharing TMI can of worms that had the potential to leave me raw. And then I might talk about the weird way I felt about Brooks. Ali didn't need that from me and I honestly didn't need it from her.

Plus, I still wasn't exactly sure what I thought about Brooks.

And Ali would want to dissect every detail and I'd have to tell her about his appearance at my window.

I pulled the string to my hoodie tighter. I had no idea how I was supposed to explain the hickey. Where it came from and how I couldn't stop staring at it, tracing my finger over it as I looked at myself in the mirror. Explanations would be a waste of time because I didn't really get him. Us. Whatever.

My phone pinged in my pocket and my body tensed at the sound. I stared at the incoming text message. Brooks. I never should've given him my number at that party in the woods. Ali looked at me in question, but I shook my head, so she hopped up and moved toward the gum-covered wall on the side of the Punkin' to talk to a bunch of the smokers leaning against it. I flipped open my phone and read the text.

Brooks: *Come to the pool tonight.*

I barked out a laugh and slid my fingers over the buttons in response.

Gannon: *Pool's closed Einstein.*

Brooks: *They don't drain it for another week. There's a swim meet or some shit.*

Gannon: *It's freezing. Swim by yourself.*

Brooks: *Meet me after.*

He was pushing me. I tucked the phone away, determined to ignore his pull. It pinged again a second later.

Brooks: *Gannon? Come on. Meet me after.*

My thumb lingered over the buttons before quickly typing.

Gannon: *Maybe.*

Brooks: *You know you want 2.*

I moved my phone back and forth between my hands. Was I really going to get into something with a moron who went illegal swimming in fifty-degree weather for fun? I thought of how many days I'd gone to bed without talking to anyone but Ali, Dennis, and Ricardo. Of how many nights I'd watched movies in my room by myself. My index finger slid over the slightly faded bruise on my neck before punching in a response.

Gannon: *Be there at 10.*

"You sure you're okay?" I asked again as Brooks navigated the streets to my house. His lips looked bluish-purple and he was gripping the steering wheel to keep his hands from shaking.

"Yep." His teeth chattered and I bit my lip.

"Not to be a bitch, but I did warn you it'd be freezing."

He pulled his light blue car to the side of the road. "Gannon. You're gonna need to stop doing that."

"Doing what?"

"Acting like you give a shit."

I opened and closed my mouth. "I—"

He faced forward and gripped the steering wheel again.

"Don't bother lying. It's true. You don't really care. You don't really know me. You're just intrigued."

I shrugged. We sat in silence for too long. "Do you want to tell me about your back?" I'd been thinking about it ever since I'd seen him at the river.

"Not really. Do you want to tell me about the cutting?"

"Nope."

He released a breath. "Okay, then."

I tapped his shoulder and pointed to the end of the street. "We're close enough. I can get out here." I moved my hand to the door handle, but he batted it away.

"I can drive you to your house," he said.

I dropped my hands to my lap and eyed the clock. My parents should be asleep, but after the argument from the other night I couldn't be sure. What would they think of Brooks?

He stopped two houses away from mine and faced me. "We're gonna be a thing, you and me."

"I don't even know you," I repeated back to him.

The thing was, I *wanted* to know him. I *was* intrigued. But it was more than that. Something I didn't even want to think about.

His fingers traced a line down my cheek. "You will, though. And I'll know you. We're gonna be good together."

"I'm a mess," I blurted out. Stupid. Too many emotions

skated along my skin when I was with him. It was like my shields didn't work against his Brooks-ness.

His laughter echoed through the car and I blinked back tears. "Oh, Gannon." His rough fingers traced my eyelids. "Don't cry. I like the mess. It makes me look better."

He leaned forward then and took my cheeks in his hands. His mouth dropped to mine, and then he really kissed me. Not a little peck or a rushed kiss like the one in the woods. A real kiss. Lips and teeth and tongue and it was so overwhelming I almost couldn't breathe. My hands tugged at his hair and I inched toward him, holding myself back from hopping into his lap. He laughed into my mouth and I let go.

He rubbed his thumb over my bottom lip and looked at me hard. "Yeah. We'll work."

He sat back into his seat. I moved on autopilot, grabbing my messenger bag and opening the door. The cool night air rushed over me, but I didn't feel it. Didn't notice my feet stumbling as I walked toward my house, knowing his eyes were on me without even turning to check. My fingers brushed over my mouth again and again. I pushed the key into the lock of the front door and finally turned back to see he was still parked in the same spot. He lifted his hand and waved at me. I waved back and then slipped into our dark front hall. My legs buckled beneath me.

I wanted to tell someone. Call Ricardo. Text Ali. Wake

my mom. But sharing wasn't my style. So I snuck up to my room and lay on my bed, staring at the ceiling. My hands slid beneath the edge of my shirt and I traced the lines carved into my stomach. And even though I knew better than to believe it, I couldn't stop the echoing of Brooks's words in my head: *We're gonna be good together.*

4

Ricardo came up to me Monday at school.

"Gannon. How come you're smiling?"

I pinched my lips together. "I'm not smiling. But what if I was?"

He grinned. Clean-cut boy grin. I had no idea why he even bothered talking to me.

"Smiling sort of works on you. Not too many teeth, just sort of nice."

I shoved him. "I'm glad you approve. Run along."

He grinned again. "Yeah. You should smile for Dennis. He'd probably have a heart attack."

I looked past Ricardo down the hall. Scanning the heads for a swatch of blue. Nothing. Stupid. We had way too many kids in our high school. But Brooks had seen me, so maybe . . .

"And off you go again," Ricardo said.

"What?"

"Into your own head. Your own world. The one you never invite anyone into."

I looked at him. "You wouldn't want to be invited in. Trust me."

He shrugged. "I could probably take it."

My eyes moved past him again. Was that blue?

His long sigh got me to turn back to him. "I'll be seeing you, Gannon."

I nodded and refocused on the books in my locker. "Yeah. Okay."

The rest of the week was annoyingly long. Brooks wasn't in school. I texted him Monday afternoon, but he said he was taking care of some things. Taking care of some things? What the hell was that supposed to mean? I stopped myself from asking for an explanation. This was the game guys played. I'd seen it with Ali dozens of times. They got all up in your head and then dropped you. I slammed around work and sneered at Ricardo for being part of the stupid asshole boy tribe.

The first few days, Brooks texted me a bunch of times. I ignored him, putting all my energy into a wooden gumball machine I was building for Alex's birthday.

The skate park had closed for the season, so when I wasn't

at work or school, I rode the El back and forth into the city to avoid going home. Most of the time I didn't get off, just sat and watched different people and wondered about their lives. The moms with small children were the most interesting to watch. Their endless diaper bags full of every little thing made me ache in a weird way. When all the time riding alone got to be too much, I made Ali ride with me.

"Do you want to go shopping?" Ali asked as she scraped the nail polish off her fingernails.

"No."

She huffed. "What do you want to do, then?"

"I don't know. Maybe see a movie?"

"Okay, but I'm not seeing one of your crappy horror movies again. That last one gave me nightmares for a week. I mean, Jesus, *Pet Sematary*? I still have to cross the street every time I see the neighbor's cat."

I laughed. "Classic."

"Can't you get into something else like romantic comedies or something?"

"God, no. Anyways, horror movies rule. I don't judge you on your choices."

She grinned at me. "That's because all of my choices are good ones. If you recall, I was the one to suggest your hair color."

I nodded. "You are a paragon of good taste." I eyed her striped tights and plaid skirt.

"Shut up. My clothes are perfect. You're just prickly because you're too short to wear any of them."

I looked at Ali's long legs and shrugged. Short legs were sort of the least of my problems.

"Okay," she said. "I have an idea. Let's go buy a bunch of *GQ*s and cut all the heads off the male models. You've been crabby all week and I know that makes you feel better."

I grinned. "Yeah. It does. Okay. I'll buy."

She clapped her hands and then reached out to squeeze my shoulder. I pulled back after a second, not wanting Ali to know how much one little squeeze meant to me. Her face broke into a smile, and it occurred to me maybe she knew anyway.

I heard Brooks before I saw him when he showed up at Standard on Friday afternoon. His heavy boots and loud voice carried through the alley.

"You ignoring me?" he said, leaning against the side of the garage.

"You had things to take care of." I flipped the power switch on the circular saw and drowned out his next few words. He strode across the garage and yanked the cord from the wall.

"What the hell?" I snapped. "Plug that back in."

He pulled me up and pressed in to me. His nipple ring rubbed against my chest and his eyes bored through me. "That's not how we play."

I pushed him off. "Oh really? How *do* we play? With you telling me we'll be good together and then disappearing? I don't think so. I don't need that shit. I'm invisible enough, thank you very much."

I bit the inside of my cheek. Why had I said that? His face softened for a second and I hated his pity so much I kicked him.

"Knock it off," he said through his teeth, stepping so close I smelled his cigarettes and soap mixed together. "Now." His hands clapped along the side of my face. "Let's get this straight: You're not invisible to me. We *will* be good together. I had some shit to take care of, but I'm not pulling you into the crap salad that's my life if I don't have to. Got me?"

I swallowed and searched his face, looking for the trick. The lie. The evidence that he didn't care. But I found only truth in his words, so I finally nodded.

"And next time I text you, you better frickin' text me back, because I know I'm not invisible to you either."

His mouth dove onto mine so fast I couldn't take a breath. His hands held me too hard and I clawed at him. He scratched me back and I moaned as I banged into the side of the garage wall. Brooks dragged his mouth away from mine and gave me a cocky smile.

"What the hell was that?" I said, breathing hard.

"I missed you."

"Funny way of showing it."

His hands slid down my back. "You liked it."

My breath hitched when he pinched the skin along my spine.

He chuckled. "Yeah. You liked it. Like I said, we'll be good together."

The movie theater in my town does "Creature Features" every Saturday night. It's how I first got into horror movies. I rarely missed one. I used to be able to talk Ali into going with me, but now I went by myself.

As I stood in the line to buy my ticket to *Freddy vs. Jason*, Brooks slid next to me.

I raised an eyebrow at him. "Are you stalking me?"

He grinned. "No. But I sort of figured you'd be here."

I stepped forward and pulled out my money. But Brooks pushed my hand back. "You're buying my ticket?"

"Yes. That's normally what happens on dates." He asked for two tickets and slipped a twenty out of his worn leather wallet.

When he had our tickets and started to usher me into the lobby, I said, "Actually, normally someone asks you on a date first."

He grinned. "That ruins the element of surprise. Admit it, you're excited I'm here. You don't have to see *Freddy vs. Jason* alone; you have someone to cling to during the scary parts."

I laughed. "I don't need anyone to cling to, thank you."

He hooked a finger in one of the belt loops on my jeans and dragged me toward him. "Well, maybe I do."

I grinned and patted his shoulder. "Okay, Brooks. I'll protect you from the scary parts."

"Outstanding. I knew this would work out."

Ease and lightness bubbled inside me. I loved Brooks like this, me like this. Normal, not broken or scarred or hurting so much I would do anything to make it all go away.

"Thanks for coming," I blurted out, then looked at my feet. Brooks tilted my chin up and searched my face. *Please don't ruin this. Don't make it more. I can't do more right now.*

"I'll go buy us some snacks," he said, and my shoulders dropped in relief. "Junior Mints okay?"

I made a face. "Junior Mints? Really? That's almost as lame as Good & Plenty. How about some popcorn?"

"Nope. Junior Mints are better."

"How do you figure that?"

He waggled his eyebrows. "Then we'll have minty fresh breath. Perfect for making out in the back of the theater."

I shook my head. "I'm here to see the movie."

He pulled me close and dropped a kiss on my lips. "Junior Mints it is."

5

My parents forced the family to go out for breakfast at the House of Pancakes on Sunday mornings. They'd tried church for a while, but it was such a ridiculous joke with my brothers they ditched the idea. The last time Father Don had seen our family, Luis had accidentally-on-purpose knocked a cup of communion wine all over him.

"So what'd you do last night?" Dad asked, one hand holding Luis firmly in his chair. Luis wiggled and picked at his pancakes with his fingers.

"Saw a movie." Just like every Saturday night. Avoided the house. Made out with Brooks.

"What movie?" Mom asked, cutting tiny bits of sausage and putting them in front of Alex.

"Mom. What're you doing? Alex is eight. He can cut his own food."

A pained expression crossed her face. "Of course he can. I was trying to be helpful."

I stared at the ceiling and counted to ten. My parents had no clue how to deal with the boys. They babied Alex, let Miguel get away with anything, and wouldn't let Luis breathe without telling him he was doing it wrong. But all of that was more attention than they'd given me for most of my teenage years. Hard to say which was worse.

My focus returned to my food, but not before I saw Miguel pluck a blueberry from his plate and throw it at Alex.

"Luis," Mom said. "Don't throw food."

Luis glared, but didn't say anything. I opened my mouth to defend him and then thought better of it. Long ago I'd learned to be quiet and either hole up in my room or get out as soon as possible. I stabbed a bite of waffle and pushed it around my plate, the sticky syrup tracing a path along the edges until several fat drops dripped off the side. Luis picked up a handful of hash browns and flung them at Mom.

Then it all started. The screaming. The stern lecture from Dad. The threats from both of them. Miguel smiled at me from across the table, picking up another blueberry and flinging it at Alex without anyone noticing. Alex started kicking the legs of the table so orange juice and water sloshed onto the vinyl tablecloth. I might have been mortified if I hadn't lived through the scene more times than I could count. I eyed the people around us and gave them my "carry on, nothing to see here" smile.

"Excuse me," I said. "I'm using the bathroom."

My parents ignored me and kept badgering Luis. I bolted toward the back of the restaurant and slipped inside the bathroom, propelling myself to the last stall. My phone found its way into my hands without me being fully aware of what I was doing. My fingers lingered over Brooks's number for only a second before pressing it.

"What are you doing?" I asked as soon as he picked up.

"Masturbating. You?"

"Gross. Forget it. I'll talk to you later."

He laughed. "Gannon. I'm messing with you. I was sleeping. What're you doing?"

"Escaping from a family breakfast by hiding in the bathroom." My voice sounded too giddy, too excited about talking to him, so I coughed.

"You want me to pick you up?" I heard rustling in the background and then a crash, followed by him swearing.

"What're you doing? Seriously."

"Jesus Christ, Gannon. It's frickin' ten thirty on a Sunday morning. What do you think I'm doing? I'm getting dressed. You woke me up."

"Oh."

"What, no apology?" I could almost hear his smirk through the phone.

"No. I don't apologize."

He laughed again and then I heard the click of a lighter. He inhaled deeply. God, a filtered menthol would go so far in making the House of Pancakes experience tolerable.

"Where are you?" he said as he exhaled.

"You can't come get me. It's Sunday breakfast. My parents have a rule."

His dark chuckle curled around me. "Yeah. I'm not so good with rules. Is there a window in there?"

I peeked out of the stall. "Yeah. It's sort of high up and it doesn't look like it opens."

"Where are you?"

"House of Pancakes."

"What side of the building is the bathroom?"

"The back. What're you thinking about doing?"

"Stay there. I'll come get you in twenty minutes."

I laughed. "I'm not staying in the bathroom for twenty minutes. It smells like the El in here."

"I don't give a shit if you stay or you don't. Just make sure you're back there in twenty minutes. I'm coming for you."

"Did you even hear me? The window doesn't look like it opens."

"Well, sweetheart," he said, "it's your lucky day. If you recall, I'm good with windows."

"But—"

"Twenty minutes. Don't disappoint me."

He clicked off and I looked at my phone. There was no way he was coming to get me. And if he was, he wouldn't be able to get through the window. But I felt better knowing he had considered it. Knowing that someone might break a window to save me from family breakfast. I shook my head. So messed up.

Things had calmed down at the table when I returned. Luis was sitting too close to Dad, wearing a sneer on his face. Alex had ordered his second meal. He did it to my parents all the time. Ordered something and refused to eat it, deciding he wanted something else. I thought they should just tell him tough shit, but my parents were psycho about Alex eating because he was basically starved when they found him in Guatemala City.

Seventeen minutes later my parents had asked for the check and were finishing up their coffee. Luis sat with his arms crossed, glaring daggers at Mom. He didn't blame Miguel for throwing the blueberries. He never blamed his brothers for anything. He protected them against the enemy, who he'd long ago decided was my parents.

"I need to go to the bathroom."

"Again?" Mom looked at me, and I shrugged. It was probably an exercise in futility, but I needed to check.

I bolted to the bathroom and hauled open the door. Brooks was standing next to the window with a smug smile on his face. I opened and closed my mouth.

"How?"

He pointed to a broken lock I hadn't noticed on the side. "Kicked it."

"You could have broken the window."

"And?" He quirked his pierced eyebrow and my feet inched toward him.

"There could've been an alarm on the window." Another step.

"At the House of Pancakes? Not likely."

I could smell his sweat mixed with lingering cigarette smoke, and somehow I didn't mind it. I shook my head to clear it and took a step back, but he grabbed me. I licked my lips and his gaze darted to my mouth.

"I need to get back to my parents," I whispered.

He shook his head. "After I've done you the courtesy of getting you out of a family breakfast? I don't think so." His arms snaked around my hips and he tugged me in to him. "You're welcome."

His mouth descended and I reached my hands into his hair, pulling him closer. His lips nipped their way down my neck until they reached the nearly faded hickey. He pushed the collar of my shirt back and sucked hard, marking me again.

Then he lifted me up and settled me on the counter before wrapping my legs around his waist.

"I need to go," I said again. This was crazy. And sort of amazing.

His fingers tightened at my hips and suddenly I was being lifted again. "Out you go, then."

I wriggled, but he gripped me harder and boosted me up to the window. I clung to the ledge and slid the window farther to the side. Then one leg after the other dropped to the ground. Brooks grunted, then hoisted himself out behind me. The screen was in pieces on the ground next to the window. I raised an eyebrow and Brooks shrugged. He pointed to his crappy Honda Civic and pushed me toward it.

"My parents—"

"Will come looking for you soon so you better get that cute ass into my car."

I'd pay for this later. My parents didn't need to be hunting me down and would freak out when I got home. But I couldn't stop myself. I watched as Brooks unlocked the passenger door. On the seat was a pack of filtered menthol cigarettes. I turned to him and he gave me a crooked smile before dropping a kiss onto my nose.

"You're welcome."

6

"Where are we going?" I asked Brooks, taking another drag off my cigarette.

"I gotta take care of something."

"You inviting me into your crap salad?" My phone buzzed in my pocket. Text from Mom. I ignored it and turned back to Brooks.

He lifted his shoulder. "Can't be helped. I didn't think I'd be seeing you today, and I gotta do something."

"That's helpful." I didn't want to be a bitch, but if I was going to have to take heat from my parents, I hoped for a bit of a game plan.

"You called me, right?"

I blew out a stream of smoke. "I didn't tell you to come get me."

He peered at me from behind his blue hair. "Then why did you call?"

I swallowed once. Twice. "What happened to your back?"

He veered his car to the side of the road, eliciting several honks and one particularly vehement hand gesture. He snatched the cigarette from my fingers and took a drag. Then he rolled down the window and spit. "Frickin' menthol."

I grinned. "Leaves your breath minty fresh. Sort of like Junior Mints."

He handed me back the cigarette and stared at me. I almost told him to forget my question, forget all the seriousness, to let me return to the ease of kisses in a dark theater. But in that moment I wanted more. I wanted to know.

"Okay." He released a breath. "So I live with an old woman. She takes a bunch of us older kids in. She has a 'no questions asked' policy about most stuff as long as we stay clean."

"Like your guardian? Are you related to her?"

"No. She's sort of like a foster mom."

I should have expected it, but it kind of surprised me. I'd never met anyone in foster care before. Did she know the reason for his scars?

I tossed the cigarette out my window. "Where are your parents?"

"Mom took off before I was two. Left everything she had, like she might come back one day. Clothes, movies, jewelry.

She was a meth head and couldn't pull her shit together. She had me too young. She was in a shitty marriage with a controlling asshole. I don't know where my dad is."

I played with the box of menthols, opening and closing the flap. "How long have you been in the foster system?"

"Five years. I've been bounced between foster care and a group home since then. Switched schools a couple times. I've got less than a year and then I'm out of the system." He pushed the hair out of his eyes and fidgeted. His other hand tapped the steering wheel. I reached out and put my hand over his. He curled his fingers around mine.

"So the scars . . ."

He looked forward and said nothing.

"I'm sorry," I whispered.

He squeezed my fingers. "Thought you didn't apologize."

His smile broke through something inside me. It was too much. I pulled back, reconstructing my defenses. I released his hand and found the cuts on my stomach. I pressed into them and the familiar bite soothed me.

His gaze zeroed in on my hand. "Don't do that. Not for me."

"It's not for you."

He yanked my hand away and shifted me closer to him. The car seemed too warm even with the windows open. I wanted another cigarette.

He locked eyes with me and didn't drop his cold expression.

"I don't want to talk about the marks on my back. They're part of the package and you don't really need to know about them."

"Did one of your fosters give them to you?"

He shook his head and stared past me out the window. Everything felt too bright, too crisp, like we shouldn't be having this conversation during the day.

"When's the last time you saw your dad?"

"Not once since I was put in the system." He paused and released a breath. "So that's all I've got for you. That's a big enough serving of the crap salad. And we're not talking about this again. Ever. Also, you owe me now."

I moved back from him. I understood what he wanted, but I wasn't ready for it. Not with him. Not with anyone. He didn't want to talk about the marks, but I was still reeling from the image of them, guessing it must have been his dad who'd beaten him.

"I owe you . . . ," I started. Only no other words came.

"I can wait," he said, and turned back to the wheel.

He screeched into traffic and turned up the radio so loud we couldn't talk. I thought about what he'd said. The tremble in his voice. His unspoken memories circling around the two of us, squeezing out all the bullshit notions of what family was supposed to be. I didn't understand everything. And I wanted him to tell me exactly what had happened to his back, but I kept my mouth shut. I lit another cigarette and stared at the mile markers along the highway.

He pulled off the ramp onto the side streets of the West Side. My parents called it the "rough neighborhood." They'd seen a news special on TV about how the West Side of Chicago had a higher crime rate than any city in the United States. Shit happened there. I wasn't stupid. But I'd heard tons of cities claiming to be the crime capital of the country and they couldn't all be the worst.

Brooks parked in front of a decaying gray-and-black house. A pit bull barked from the gate on the side.

"I'll be right back."

"What? Where are you going?"

He sighed. "I told you, I have to take care of something."

"And you're leaving me in the car? Hell no. I'm not some trophy girl waiting for her guy while he takes care of business."

He raised an eyebrow, the barbell reaching toward his forehead. "You want to come in?"

My gaze shifted to the crappy-looking house and the pit bull. I lifted my chin. "Yes."

"Suit yourself." He leaned over me and shoved my door open.

I stepped out and looked at the house again. The paint had peeled off on most of one side. The steps leading up to the front door were covered in gang-symbol graffiti. Crap. What the hell had I gotten myself into?

Brooks climbed up the steps without even checking to see

if I was following. He banged on the door and a guy in a dirty white T-shirt opened it. He nodded at Brooks and pulled the door open wider. I stepped in and saw six guys sitting around a table, smoking a bong. The house was dark and hazy, navy blue sheets covering the windows. I couldn't really see the details of the guys' faces. They looked at me for less than a second before turning their attention back to the bong. The air reeked of weed, and the walls were covered in weird African print pictures.

"Where's Kenji?" Brooks asked.

The guy who opened the door nodded to the back of the house and snagged the bong from a dreadlocked white guy wearing no shirt. Brooks grabbed my elbow and steered me to a back room.

"Kenji," he yelled, banging on a door with LEGALIZE POT stickers all over it. He turned the knob and pushed himself in.

Kenji and a too-skinny white woman lay naked on a bed. Neither of them moved to cover themselves when we entered. Kenji smiled and I noticed he was missing a few of his front teeth. He was tall and wiry, his dark skin ashy as if he could use a bath in a vat of lotion. Holy hell, what was I doing here?

"Brooks. My man." Kenji stood up and I dropped my gaze. Very few things fazed me to the point of reaction, but uncircumcised penises were a bit much right after breakfast.

Kenji and Brooks did a complicated handshake and I

looked at the skinny white woman. She was more of a girl, really. Probably not much older than me. Her eyes were glazed over. She didn't appear to register us entering the room.

"I'm here for Ray's package. You got it?"

Kenji turned around and started to rifle through his drawers. I elbowed Brooks and signaled to Kenji's bare ass. Brooks smirked at me.

"There you go," Kenji said, turning back to us. "Tell him it's the good stuff and he owes me."

Kenji handed a bag of white powder to Brooks. My mouth dropped open. Drug run? What the hell? I ditched breakfast for this?

Kenji nodded to me. "Your girl want a sample?"

"No," Brooks answered before I could even open my mouth.

Kenji's eyes darted between the two of us. He raised his eyebrows but then shrugged. "If you change your mind, lovely, you know where to find me."

Brooks stepped in front of me. "She won't."

The two of them did some sort of silent communication with each other and I eyed the door. *Please get me out of here.*

Brooks steered me out of the room. "I'll give Ray the message," he said over his shoulder.

We moved toward the front of the house. One of the six guys stood when he saw us and maneuvered himself against the front door. He was massive, more like a professional wrestler than a stoner. His body blocked any chance of exit.

"How much for your girl?" He stared at me. My arms curled across my chest and I took a tiny step toward Brooks. *Crapcrapcrapcrap.*

Brooks paused for less than a beat. "She's infected."

My stomach clenched. What?

Gigantor's eyes roved over me and I thought I might barf. "Yeah?" he said. "With what?"

"Herpes and HIV."

I opened my mouth. Brooks's eyes darted to mine and he gave a tiny shake of his head.

Gigantor stepped to the side. "Nah. Not worth it. Half the people I know have HIV, but herpes is a bitch to get rid of. Sorry, girlie. You woulda had fun with me."

I blinked back angry tears and stepped out of the house. As soon as we got inside Brooks's car, I turned on him.

"You took me to a crack house and almost sold me? What the hell?"

He shrugged. "I wouldn't have sold you. That's why I told him you were infected."

"Couldn't you just have tried 'no'?"

He shook his head. "Nope. I've tussled with him before. It's not worth it. Sure, I'd win, but I wouldn't come out unscathed. Easier this way."

"Easier to let him think I was infected?"

He turned to me. "Gannon. Why do you care what a bunch of guys in a crack house think?"

I shook my head and faced forward. My hands reached for another cigarette. Brooks snatched it from my fingers.

"Enough with the menthols. I didn't think you were gonna smoke the whole pack in one morning. You're stinking up my car."

I crossed my arms. "Take me home."

"No."

"Take me home."

"No. I have a plan. Trust me. You'll like it."

Trust him? He'd just taken me into a crack house. How was this trustworthy behavior? Even if I was the one who'd insisted on going in with him.

"You were the one who wouldn't wait in the car," he said, and I punched him for knowing what I was thinking.

He didn't even flinch, just traced his fingers over the hickey on my neck. "Come on. I'm sorry. Please. Trust me."

I released a breath. My moods around him were all over the place, but still, it was better than being home for the afternoon with my brothers. Sad as that sounded. I finally nodded and offered up a silent prayer that I wouldn't regret my choice.

After we'd been driving fifteen minutes with nothing but

loud music between us, I couldn't squelch my curiosity any longer. I switched the radio off and faced him. "I take it you've been to that house before?"

Brooks shrugged. "A few times. I'm not into crack, if that's what you're worried about."

I was, but I wasn't about to tell him that. "I've never been to a place like that."

Brooks snorted and the bar in his eyebrow moved up and down. "I figured. It's not *exactly* a crack house. It used to be Kenji's aunt's place before she died. Those are just some of the guys he hangs out with."

"And Kenji's a dealer?"

"Yep."

So it *was* a crack house. I took a deep breath. "Drugs aren't really my thing. I've tried pot, but that's kind of it."

Brooks didn't respond. His hands gripped the steering wheel and he turned onto Lake Shore Drive.

"This would be the time when you tell me drugs aren't really your thing either."

He barked out a bitter laugh. "What do you want me to say? I've been in the foster care system a long time. Kenji was seventeen when I first got in it, living in a group home because his aunt was too sick to take care of him. I met him. I liked him. I'm not an addict, but the last few years would've sucked without him."

I bit my lip. How could I even begin to understand Brooks's life?

He glanced at me sideways. "I don't come in a perfect package, Gannon. Perfect is boring."

I leaned my head against the window and stared at the boats in the harbor. The desire for numb swept over me and I squeezed my eyes shut, wishing for the safety of my razors and the oblivion they brought. My hands fisted and unfisted. Brooks reached over and pulled the hair on the back of my neck. Relief passed over me for too short a time before his grip loosened. I reached for his hand, forcing him to grab a bigger chunk of my hair, and then jerked forward, leaving him holding a fistful of dark strands.

Brooks looked between the road, my face, and the loose strands. Then he startled me by letting out a belly laugh. He dropped the hair onto the floor and squeezed my thigh too hard before patting me.

Still smiling, he winked at me and said, "That's my girl."

I smiled back and leaned my head against the seat, the pain in my scalp uncoiling the overwhelming emotions in the pit of my stomach.

7

"You're taking me to the zoo?" I eyed the Lincoln Park Zoo sign and pursed my lips.

"Oh, Christ no. Poor animals. It's worse than juvie."

I exhaled. I hated zoos. They were almost as depressing as the circus. My parents tried to encourage me to take part in their family outings to these places, but after I read the sign about the seal dying because too many assholes had thrown coins and pop tops into the pool and he'd ingested them, they stopped making me go.

Brooks pulled me out of the passenger seat and gripped my hand. The phone in my pocket buzzed for the tenth time. Mom, demanding I come home. I'd texted her after we left Kenji's, but she was still pissed and "worried." This really meant she needed a referee for her fight with the boys. Dad would already be in the tiny windowless corner room in the basement, pretending to work but really watching football too loud, avoiding all of it.

About nine months ago after Luis was suspended for fighting, Dad had started to withdraw from our family life. I could tell by how late he worked, how early he left in the mornings, and how much he pretended the boys weren't a problem. It was like something cracked and he gave up. He'd been an insurance broker for years. Sudden late nights should have been a red flag for Mom. But she was worn down and didn't want to admit the toll the boys had taken on the two of them. She refused to even acknowledge the dysfunction in our family. She couldn't give the boys back, although once, in the heat of a particularly nasty argument with Luis, I'd heard her threaten it.

"You're gonna like this," Brooks promised again, squeezing my hand.

I dragged my feet, unsure of what constituted a fun date in Brooks's mind. He wrapped his arm around my neck and tugged me closer. We approached the tiny pond by the north entrance of the zoo. He gave me a widemouthed grin and pointed to several paddleboats lined up along the edge of the pond. I raised a brow at him.

"Paddleboats?"

His boy grin lit up his face and I had to tamp down my impulse to jump him. "Yeah. Pretty romantic, eh?" He wagged his eyebrows and I snorted.

"It might be if it wasn't closed on Sunday." I pointed to the sign that listed the limited fall hours.

His fingers tickled the edge of my ear and he leaned closer to me. "I think I might've already mentioned this," he whispered, and I shivered slightly. "But closed signs aren't really a deterrent for me."

He lifted me off the ground and dropped me over the low wooden fence by the pond.

"Someone might see us." I glanced around at the joggers on the nearby path. "This isn't exactly a private spot."

"And?" He hopped over after me and made his way to the line of paddleboats.

I shut my mouth. There wasn't going to be any talking Brooks out of this. His eyes buzzed like a little boy who wouldn't leave the amusement park until he got to ride the roller coaster. He approached the last paddleboat in line and tried to push it away from the others. A chintzy bike lock held it in place. I bit back a laugh. Brooks grinned at me and pulled a Leatherman tool from his pocket. He squeezed the lock between the pliers and then jumped on the tool as hard as he could. Both the lock and the tool broke.

"Son of a bitch. I just got that," he said, picking up the broken Leatherman. He shook his head and snatched the lock from the boat. "Your chariot." He gestured to the paddleboat and I took a small step forward.

"You're not afraid of the water, are you?" His voice sounded almost disappointed.

I shook my head.

"Thank Christ for that. I'd hate to lose a Leatherman for nothing."

Before I could even respond, he grabbed my elbow and shoved me into the boat. I wiggled a little, squirming to avoid the puddle of water between the seats. Brooks hopped into the boat after me, kicking us off the side of the dock. His long legs pedaled the boat backward while he steered with a handle in the middle. I tried to pedal, but my feet kept slipping. Finally Brooks batted them away. Several people saw us and pointed, but they didn't seem to care that we were doing something illegal. The cool fall air tickled my face. I shut my eyes, tilted my head back, and let the lingering warmth of the sun calm me.

"I was right," Brooks said after he'd pedaled us toward the center of the pond. "It's fun, isn't it?"

I opened my eyes and smiled at him. "It's fun."

He stopped pedaling. "So tell me about your brothers."

Four guys jogging past shouted something to us, but I couldn't hear what they said. Brooks flipped them off and turned back to me. "Your brothers?"

"Yeah. Luis, Miguel, and Alex. Eleven, nine, and eight. There isn't a lot to say. My parents got them too late. They'd been on the streets in Guatemala too long. Mom and Dad could have helped Alex, maybe, if he'd been on his own, but there was no hope with all three." I searched the pocket of my hoodie for my cigarettes but remembered I'd left them in the car. My fingers itched for something to do. Brooks grabbed my hands and sandwiched them between his.

"So when did they adopt them?"

"Five years ago."

He studied my face. I looked past him, the edges of me starting to blur into numbness.

"And when did you disappear?" he asked after the space between us had grown too large.

I bit the inside of my cheek and kept my mouth shut. He released my hands and pulled me onto his lap. It was awkward and uncomfortable in the paddleboat, but he held tight. I leaned in to him, tucking my head against his chest, unwilling to face any pity from him.

"Gannon? When did you disappear?"

"About then," I whispered.

He shifted me back and lifted my chin. His thumb traced the edge of my jaw. "That's why you cut?"

I shrugged. It wasn't exactly the reason, but it was good enough. I couldn't explain it any other way. Brooks couldn't understand the way it made me feel, even if he understood I needed it. It relieved an unbearable pressure inside me. Which sounded psychotic even to me, and I was the one living it.

His mouth descended on mine and it felt like he wanted to swallow me whole. I could barely breathe, but I didn't want it to stop. His hands roved over me, sliding down the curve of my hips and back up to the cuts on the sides of my stomach. I wrapped my arms around his neck and pressed into him, feeling his sinewy muscles over his thin frame.

"Hey! Hey!" a voice from behind us shouted.

I pulled back, breathing hard.

Brooks's gaze drifted past me. "Damn." He nudged me from his lap and started pedaling fast. I whipped my head around. A short Asian man was standing by the other paddleboats, waving his arms at us.

"Who's that?"

"Owner of the paddleboats, I guess," Brooks said as he steered us to the bank on the opposite side of the pond.

"Crap." I shifted forward and joined his frantic pedaling.

Brooks barked out a maniacal laugh. His feet slowed and I belted him. He laughed even harder.

"I'm not getting busted for this," I said through my teeth.

He started to pedal fast again. "Neither am I."

He steered our boat to the edge of the pond and I leaped out. He followed, still laughing but moving quickly. The boat started to drift back into the pond, and Brooks grabbed my hand and pushed me toward the running path. The sound of sirens echoed in the distance and I ran faster. Brooks maneuvered us into the center of a group of runners.

"Let's cut through the zoo," he said.

I gritted my teeth and moved with him past the zoo entrance. We stopped running and Brooks pointed to a bench. I plopped down and crossed my arms. He laughed again and dropped his arm behind me.

"That was fun," he said, breathing hard.

"Yeah. Not so much."

"Oh, come on, sweetheart. That was fun. You loved it. Admit it."

"No." I shifted away from him. "So far today you've taken me to a crack house and nearly gotten me arrested. This is hardly gaining you boyfriend points."

"Boyfriend, eh?" He slid closer to me. "I didn't think you were ready for that, but I'm in." His fingers traced the hickey on my neck.

"I—"

He put his fingers over my mouth. "Don't ruin it by saying something stupid."

"Go to hell."

He laughed. "Is that a girlfriend term of endearment?"

I clamped my mouth shut.

He launched himself off the bench and held his hand out to me. "I should probably take you home now."

The day hadn't been anything like I'd expected and I still wasn't sure if dealing with my parents' anger was worth it, but as Brooks pulled me up and brushed another kiss on my lips, part of me decided it might be.

Brooks parked in my driveway despite my insistence that he should leave me on the corner. He stepped out of the car and came to my side, his fingers linking with mine. Most of the time I was embarrassed about the state of my house when people came over. It needed a face-lift in the worst way, but as Dad liked to point out, kids are expensive, and because of my brothers Mom refused to work anytime but half-day mornings as an assistant at a preschool. No money, crap house. Fortunately, Brooks had experienced every kind of living situation, and after seeing Kenji's place I wasn't so worried.

Mom opened the door before we'd even reached the first step. Her mouth dropped open when she saw Brooks. I doubted it was his blue hair; she'd gotten used to crazy hair with my zebra stripes. She'd just never seen me with a boy who wasn't Ricardo before. And Ricardo never held my hand.

"It was my fault," Brooks said before she recovered from the shock. I looked at him and he winked at me. "I wanted to see her and I wouldn't let her go until she went to the zoo with me. I'm a horrible influence. I'm Michael, by the way. I'd like to date your daughter." He flashed a boyish grin at Mom, and I thought I heard her sigh. Holy crap, Brooks was good with moms.

She blinked a few times and then narrowed her eyes at me. "How did you get out of the restaurant?"

"I work there," Brooks interrupted. "My shift was over and I saw her and insisted she come with me."

Mom crossed her arms. "You could have told us."

I opened my mouth to speak, although I didn't have anything to say. Before I could stammer out a bogus explanation, Luis screamed from the background. Miguel squealed and something broke. Mom whipped around and took a step into the house. She turned back to me.

"I need your help."

Resentment pricked along the back of my neck, but I nodded and released Brooks's hand. She shook her head at Brooks, but in this weird sort of girlish way.

"Michael. It's nice to meet you. Come here first next time."

Then she bolted into the house. I smiled at Brooks and shrugged. He dropped a kiss onto my nose and pinched my ass as I walked away. I whacked him in the arm, but he only gave me another innocent grin.

"See you in school."

The door clicked behind me and I leaned against it for a second. I shut my eyes and pictured Brooks's face, hidden on one side by his blue hair. My fingers touched the mark on my neck again and I adjusted my hoodie to hide it. I peeked out the window on the side of the door and watched Brooks slide into his car. The word popped into my head before I could shut it down, and my insides melted at the truth behind it: *Mine*.

8

Wood shop was my last class of the day and the only one I consistently got an A in. I was a C student in everything else. I probably could have gotten better grades, but it was more trouble than it was worth. Especially since the sad reality was I probably *would* end up working for Dennis the rest of my life. Although, hopefully, I'd live in the yet-to-be-renovated apartment above the store instead of with my psycho brothers.

Most of the time we worked independently in the shop studio, but today my teacher decided to give us a lesson in scale drawing. I hated the drawing part of shop and thought it might be the thing that kept me from doing anything real with my carpentry skills. Everything I sketched looked like a mis-shapen foot, and the guys in class had no problem relentlessly teasing me about it. Probably because no one could get near my excellence with the jigsaw.

I fumbled with my pencils, cursing three-dimensional design under my breath.

"Psst. Gannon."

I looked up and raised a brow. Rodney, one of the work-study kids, leaned closer to me.

"I heard you're dating that guy with the blue hair?"

I shrugged. "So?"

"How long you been dating him?"

"I don't know. Why?" People were talking about me? Weird.

"I heard he's got a record."

Oh. That explained it. Speculation on time spent in juvie was like cotton candy to a diabetic in the high school gossip circles. Ali constantly updated me on which guys at the Punkin' were rumored to have been locked up. It was all bullshit.

"So?" I said with a sigh.

"So you're dating a guy with a record."

I tapped the pencil on my desk. "Rodney, I'm not exactly one to follow rumors, you know?"

He sucked his lower lip through his teeth, drawing attention to our conversation with his disgusting slurping sound. Jeremy, the guy who sat behind me and never talked about anything but playing StarCraft, poked my shoulder.

"I heard that too. From a pretty reliable source."

"Yeah?" I tapped my chin. "Who would that be? One of your online pals?"

He sneered at me. "As a matter of fact, I play with one of the guys who lives with him. He said Brooks has been to juvie. He killed a guy or something."

I snorted. "Give me a break. How would he be in school if he killed a guy?"

Our teacher stood up and gave us the Jedi death stare. I bit my lip and went back to my drawing.

"Just watch your back," Rodney whispered from my side. I shook my head and ignored the doubt prickling along the base of my neck.

"Where've you been lately?" Ali asked as I pulled books from my locker and shoved them into my messenger bag.

"Do you care?" I scratched at the plaid skirt rubbing against my fishnets and wondered again if jeans would have been an easier choice.

Ali flashed her tongue barbell and grinned. "Only if it's somewhere good."

I laughed. "No. Nowhere good. Just around. Avoiding home."

Ali nodded. "Wanna talk about it?"

"Nope."

She tilted her head and looked at me hard. I turned away

so she wouldn't see the hickey and added another book to my bag.

"So you haven't asked me about Jace yet," she finally said.

"The guy from the woods? What about him?"

"Hot, right?"

I shrugged. No blue hair. No eyebrow stud. He wasn't Brooks. "Where'd you meet him again?"

"I told you before. Dark Alley."

I groaned. Buying clothes at poseur, overpriced hipster shops like Dark Alley was almost as bad as getting music from the "What's Hot" section of Walmart.

"What were you doing at Dark Alley?"

"I saw him through the window. He works there." She clicked her tongue piercing. "I know, it's lame or whatever, but he gets an employee discount and they have really cool vintage stuff."

Really cool vintage stuff like the same I'M A PEPPER seventies retro T-shirt on the racks at Urban Outfitters? I bit my tongue and adjusted the strap on my bag. It wasn't my business who Ali spent time with.

"So what'd you do yesterday?"

I smiled for a half second, then slammed the door to my locker. "Family breakfast."

Ali hooked her arm in mine and started walking me down the hall. "Did they kick your family out of the House of Pancakes again?"

"Not exactly."

"Oh my God, they didn't call the police, did they? Remember when Luis told the barista at Starbucks his mom had abandoned him? And when she asked who the woman with him was, he told her she was a stranger who kept wanting him to get in her car?"

"Yeah," I said, laughing. "My mom had to pull out family photos to prove he actually was hers. I told her she should have left him."

Ali snorted. "She probably would have been better off."

Comfortable silence slid between us. A bunch of people said hi to Ali as we passed, but they mostly ignored me.

"So are you working this afternoon?" she asked, hitching her bag on her shoulder.

I nodded, turning down the hall toward the exit.

"Well, call me later, okay? I really want you to meet Jace."

"Yeah, sure, whatever."

She pursed her lips to say something, but then shook her head.

Did she expect me to get enthusiastic about a guy named Jace? What a stupid name. It was like a combination of "jackass" and "ace." Not that I was any kind of expert on guys, but Ali could do so much better than someone who worked at Dark Alley. I pushed my mouth into a smile, waved to her, and headed out the door. My feet scraped along the sidewalk as the bitter breeze cut across my face. Tears stung the corner of my eyes, and I wondered if maybe I should bust into my hardware money to get a car. I smiled at the thought of Brooks in his crappy Honda. Maybe I wouldn't need my own car.

Ricardo was in front messing with the window display again. He stood holding six plastic pumpkins and a sack of fake leaves. I was at the main counter while Dennis barked orders at Ricardo to adjust the scarecrow.

"We're a hardware store. What do we need a Halloween display for?"

Ricardo added, "Yeah, Dennis, don't you think—"

Dennis cut him off. "I *do* think, so you all don't have to. I'm not paying you for your opinions."

Ricardo exchanged a glance with me and shrugged. We knew Dennis well enough not to be affected by his bluster. We'd both seen enough little bonuses in our paychecks to know he was grateful for how much we did for the store.

"Now put more leaves to the left there," Dennis said.

Ricardo sighed and opened the leaf bag with his teeth.

A crash came from the back door and Brooks toppled in. "There's my girl," he said too loud, with a slur.

My eyes widened and I looked at Dennis. He squinted and curled his mouth downward. Crap. Drunk Brooks, just what I needed.

"Friend of yours?" Dennis asked.

I nodded and bolted to the back of the store, trying to get to Brooks before he got any closer to Dennis. Brooks wrapped his arms around me in an awkward hug when I reached him, leaning in to me for support.

"You've been drinking," I said in a low voice.

He grabbed my cheeks and dropped a sloppy kiss on my lips. I sputtered and stepped back. He'd apparently been bathing in peppermint schnapps.

"Detention without a flask is like a fish without a bicycle . . . or something," he slurred.

I snorted. "If you're gonna quote Gloria Steinem, get it right." I yanked his arm from around me and dragged him toward the back door. "Be right back, Dennis," I called over my shoulder.

Dennis shook his head and went back to barking orders at Ricardo.

I pushed Brooks out the door into the back alley. He stumbled a few times before steadying himself on my shoulder.

"You were in detention like this?"

"They didn't even notice." He tripped and landed hard on his ass. I stood with my hands on my hips.

"What are you doing here?"

He stayed on the ground. "I had detention."

"No, what are you doing here? At my work?"

He gave me a crooked smile, but I didn't react. "I told you I'd see you in school. But I didn't, couldn't find you, so I came for you."

"Where's your car? You didn't drive here, did you?"

"No. It's at school."

Well, there was that at least. "You're pathetic. Who gets wasted at Monday detention?"

A strange look crossed his face, but then he grinned again. "Me. Apparently. You want some?" He pulled a flask out of his back pocket. It had a flamenco dancer on it and seemed almost feminine. I stifled a groan.

"I'm working until six. And even if I weren't, I'm not drinking on a Monday afternoon. I have to go home to my family."

As soon as I said the words, I regretted them. Brooks flinched and pushed himself off the ground. "My mistake. I'll see you."

He turned his back on me and tottered forward. Part of me wanted to stop him, sober him up, and take him home. But the other part of me, the bigger part, was too overwhelmed to deal with any of his shit. He walked away, zigzagging across the sidewalk, and I returned to Ricardo and Dennis.

I didn't get home until almost eight. Dennis got this idea to hang pumpkin lights all over the store and had us try all these different arrangements before he made up his mind to scrap it and stick to just decorating the front window. Ricardo asked if I wanted to go for pizza, but I turned him down. I was still smarting from the disappointment of Brooks's drunken appearance.

Halfway down my block, Luis and Miguel came tearing past me. They'd teamed up this time; I could tell by the pace they kept. Mom's voice carried from the house: "Get back here right now, both of you." Her words cracked at the end. Whatever the hell they'd done, it was bad.

I motored to the front door and saw her standing with a ball of fluff in her hand. An unmoving ball of fluff. My feet refused to take the last few steps toward her.

"What is that?"

Her gaze darted between the end of the block and her hands before finally landing on my face.

"What is that?" I asked again.

"The Wilsons' new kitten."

Such a huge wave of grief hit me I almost crumpled where I stood. I shut my eyes. "Oh my God, what did they do?"

Her hands shook. "What do you think they did? They killed it. Kicked it. Stepped on it. I didn't even know until I heard them laughing in the backyard."

Every muscle in my body protested, but I stepped forward and took the kitten from her. It was warm, but so still and limp I almost dropped it. "Go get the boys. I'll take care of the cat."

I moved past her into the house, dropping my bag onto the

floor and shifting the kitten onto the newspaper sitting on the side table. Alex watched me with large eyes and a trembling mouth. I blinked back tears.

"Don't be like them," I said quietly. It was a stupid command. Alex couldn't change his fate any more than I could. In a few years he'd be running right along with his brothers.

I picked up the cat and moved toward the back door, flicking on the floodlights with my elbow. Mom's forgotten compost pile was in the back corner of the garden, and I made my way to it quickly, pretending I wasn't carrying the neighbor boy's pride and joy in my arms.

I dropped to my knees, set the kitten down, and grabbed the tiny shovel next to the compost. Dirt pricked my knees through the holes in my fishnets. The ground was too hard; only small pieces of dirt flung up when I tried to pierce it. My hands shook and I adjusted my grip on the shovel. I tried breathing through my mouth, but my entire body started to tremble. I gulped in a huge breath of air, squeezing my eyes so tight my head throbbed. How could they? And why was I somehow not surprised? I sat there too long, swallowing down the sobs that pressed against the back of my throat until my head hurt. Something moved behind me and I swiveled, ready to send Alex back inside.

Brooks. A whimper escaped from me and then he was there with his arms around me, cradling me as I sobbed into his chest. His hands brushed over my hair and he still smelled a bit like schnapps, but it didn't matter. He was there and held me like my own parents hadn't done in too many years to count.

When my sobs turned to sniffles, Brooks lifted me from his lap and finished digging the hole. He slid the kitten in and covered her. He balled the newspaper up and tossed it in the compost pile. Then he took me back in his arms and squeezed me. His leather bracelet irritated my skin, but I didn't move away. I wanted the pain. Needed it.

Brooks stood up and grabbed my hand, helping me to my feet. He steered us in through the back door. Mom was there, eyes red and hollow at the same time. The boys were sitting at the kitchen table, eating but not saying a word. I wanted to throw up.

Brooks led me past them, said something in a low voice to my mom, and guided me upstairs. She didn't register us leaving the kitchen. I glanced out the front window and saw Dad's car in the driveway. He was home and in hiding. I hated him so much. Hated all of them.

Brooks clicked the door to my bedroom shut and twisted the lock. He signaled me to lie on the bed. Tears threatened to spill again, but he pulled my shirt off and guided his fingers over the cuts crisscrossing my stomach. If he noticed there were more, he didn't say anything. Just traced them softly before meeting my eyes in question. I looked away. I couldn't say what I wanted, but somehow he knew, because suddenly his fingers were digging into my skin, reopening scabbed-over wounds. My body buckled in pain and relief.

After it was over, Brooks slipped into my bathroom and rifled through drawers until he found bandages. He kissed the cuts and scars on my torso before cleaning them off and covering them. I loved him then. For all of it. And I fell asleep against the plane of his chest, soothed by the touch of his fingers tracing the hoops along my ear.

9

When I woke to the first rays of light pouring through my window, Brooks was gone. I rubbed the sleep from my eyes and dragged myself into the shower. My hands skimmed over the bandages on my stomach before quickly ripping them off. One of my cuts started to bleed again and the soap stung as it passed over it, but I didn't care. I turned the water up as high as I could take it and shut my eyes against the events of the past day.

Mom was sitting at the kitchen table, twirling a cup of coffee in her hands, when I walked downstairs. I poured a bowl of corn flakes and sat across from her.

"Sorry about yesterday."

I nodded.

"I don't know what I'm going to tell the Wilsons."

The spoon dropped from my hand. "You haven't told them anything yet?"

She shook her head and I felt sick. Poor Tim was probably freaking out.

"I couldn't. What am I supposed to say?"

Your kids are messed up and belong in a detention facility? I almost said it out loud but shoveled another spoonful of corn flakes into my mouth instead.

"Maybe," she continued, "I could tell them the cat was hit by a car."

I gaped at her. "You're thinking about lying?"

She twirled her coffee mug faster and nodded. "You wouldn't understand, but sometimes lying is really the kindest option."

The legs of my chair scraped along the floor as I got up and dropped my bowl into the sink. I grabbed my messenger bag and took off without saying another word. *You wouldn't understand, but sometimes lying is really the kindest option.* Her words bounced around in my head. I understood perfectly. And the pathetic part was that she had no clue I was a living example of that.

"You okay?" Brooks's voice whispered along the back of my neck, and I bit my lip to stop the grin threatening to blossom.

I turned from my locker and nodded. "Yeah. I guess." My

hands itched to reach for him so I tucked them into my jeans pockets. "Thanks."

"Sorry about yesterday," he said.

I looked at him sideways and he motioned like he was drinking. So much had happened; I'd almost forgotten about his performance at the store.

"Don't do it again. My job, Dennis, Ricardo, they're the only things I care about. Don't mess that up. I don't want to be fired."

He stepped closer and my breath caught. "The only things?" Heat burned my cheeks as he dipped down and nibbled his favorite spot on my neck.

I curled closer to him. "Not the only things," I whispered.

Before I could lean farther in to him, he pushed me against my locker and gripped my hips tightly. He drove his tongue into my mouth and I squeaked a little. Watching hallway PDA used to represent the worst form of torture for me, but everything was different with Brooks. I couldn't release him, couldn't get enough of him.

"Get a room," someone yelled, and I finally pulled back.

Brooks's eyes buzzed with energy and I imagined I didn't look much more composed. We'd just declared ourselves a couple to the whole high school. And while most of them didn't care about me, Brooks was the new kid and the cause of a great deal of speculation.

"I won't be able to come over later," he said, and I hated

the crushing feeling in my stomach. "But later this week, okay? I'll bring over a movie. Maybe *Fright Night*."

"Where are you gonna be?"

He released a sigh and pushed the hair out of his face. The black T-shirt he had on looked like it hadn't been washed in a week. "You weren't the only one pissed about my schnapps intake yesterday. My foster mom is making me go to AA every day this week."

I burst into laughter. "Really? Do you have to get a sponsor and everything?"

"No. I already have one. They made me get one in rehab."

My laughter stopped. "Oh."

He leaned in and tugged at the hoops in my ear. "Don't look so surprised, sweetheart. It was a long time ago, and now it's all part of my rock-and-roll image."

I opened my mouth to ask him about the rumors of him in juvie, but before I could say anything, he dropped a kiss on my lips and moved into the hordes of people walking down the hall. "Saturday, though," he called back to me. "I'll come for you Saturday."

Saturday couldn't come soon enough. Although I saw Brooks in the halls and even managed to let him feel me up during Thursday lunch hour, it wasn't the same as being with him outside school.

Things at home were strange and quiet. I had no idea what Mom had said to the Wilsons, but I'd seen Tim playing outside with a new puppy on Friday morning. My brothers exchanged glances a lot, but none of them had had any more psychotic episodes since the kitten. The circles beneath Mom's eyes were so prominent they looked like bad makeup. Dad talked at all of us, worked late, and pretended everything was fine.

"So Tim's got a new dog," Dad said during our particularly excruciating Friday-night dinner. "Seems like everything is fine there."

Mom coughed but then covered with her cheery voice. "Yes. He seems really happy about it."

"I'm surprised he didn't get another cat." My dad, the huge asshole.

Everything stilled. Not even plate clinking or cup scraping from the boys.

Dad met my eyes across the table, then looked down. "Although maybe not," he mumbled.

After a completely word-free dessert, I made two deep cuts on my inner thighs. Brooks's face flashed into my mind and guilt nipped at me, but I couldn't stand the painful silence blanketing my house any longer.

Brooks hadn't mentioned a game plan for our date other than for me to be ready to be retrieved at eight o'clock. *Retrieved.*

His word choice. I slid a cutoff jean skirt over my fishnets and tugged on my black leather boots. I threw on a long-sleeve T-shirt with two tanks layered over the top. I applied too much makeup and grinned at myself in the mirror. Just right for my blue-haired boy.

My parents had taken the boys to the movies because they'd had a "good week" following the kitten disaster. It was all ridiculous make-believe and I ignored them when they left. I was standing at my mirror fussing over my hair when I heard Brooks scream from the front porch.

"Gannon. Gannon."

I peeked out the window and waved to him.

"Get your hot little self down here before I drag you out of the house."

I bolted down the stairs and pulled him inside. "What the hell are you doing? I have neighbors, and my parents could have been home."

He gave me a boyish grin and checked me out. "You look edible."

"Gross." I swatted him.

"I peeked into the garage," he said. "Your parents' car was gone. And I don't give a shit about your neighbors. At this point I'm sure they've already designated this the House of Crazy."

I shivered at the memory of Tim Wilson's dead kitten.

Brooks pulled me toward him and dropped tiny kisses all

over my face. His hands slid down to my thighs and tucked into my jean skirt pockets. "This I like."

I drew back from him, scared of the want that overtook me whenever he got close. "Where are we going tonight?"

"A party."

I raised an eyebrow. "That's your big date plan? Take me to a party? You promised me *Fright Night.*"

He lifted one hand and skimmed his fingers over the faded hickey on my neck, frowning. "Some other time. There's a good band playing. Most of your Punkin' Donuts friends will be there. And I guarantee you won't regret what you do with me tonight."

I slipped out of his arms and took a step back. "The Punkin' Donuts crew are not my friends. They're poseurs who shop at Urban Outfitters and Dark Alley. The only thing they're good for is bumming cigarettes, and most of them don't smoke menthols. Also, you should probably hold off on making me any guarantees of fun. You're not exactly batting a thousand in that area."

His fingers hooked into the neck of one of my tank tops and he tugged me toward him. He dropped to his knees and raised the bottom of my shirts to expose my stomach, searching for new cuts. I looked away. His tongue found one of my scars and circled it.

"But I'm not exactly a total failure, either, eh?" he said through licks.

I yanked my shirt down. The room had gotten too hot. I pulled him off his knees and led him toward the door.

The night was cool, but the goose bumps on my neck felt more like anticipation than a reaction to the weather. He opened the passenger door of his rusty Civic and booked around to his side, bouncing in excitement. He peeled out of my driveway, waving at Tim and his new puppy playing on the front lawn next door. He turned on the radio and opened his glove compartment to a package of filtered menthols. I smiled at him and patted his head before pulling out the pack and lighting up.

Two cigarettes and a lecture about why I should roll my own smokes later, we'd pulled up to a fancy house on the edge of Thatcher Woods. I stubbed my cigarette out and put the butt into the box.

"Do you trust me?" Brooks asked, flicking on the light inside the car.

"No."

He laughed. "Good."

He'd replaced his eyebrow bar with a ring, and little butterflies popped up in my stomach at the strange sexiness of him. His dark eyes searched my face and then he pulled a small piece of paper from his back pocket.

He unfolded it and revealed two tiny blue pills with clovers stamped on them.

"E?"

He nodded and popped one into his mouth, chewing slowly.

I inched back, shaking my head. "Pass."

He grabbed my hand and pressed the pill into it. "You won't regret it," he whispered.

"I'm not having sex with you tonight."

He looked me over and nodded. "Okay. But still take it. I don't want to be the only one."

"You should have asked me."

His hand dropped to my thigh and he squeezed. "Sorry. But I promise it'll be fun."

I gnawed at my lip. "I've never done it before."

"You'll like it. Probably too much. But I'll keep an eye on you."

"I don't know about this. E isn't exactly the most consistent drug, you know? Ali's taken it a bunch of times and it's never really the same. Plus, I've told you, drugs aren't my thing."

He moved his fingers up and tugged at a bleached section of my hair. "I know. You said. But you'll like this one. I promise."

It was seven million kinds of stupid. Only somehow, being with Brooks, I didn't care. I didn't trust him, but I didn't care what happened because it would be okay. Not perfect, not legal, but okay. I popped the pill in my mouth and leaned my head back against the headrest of my seat as I chewed away at the bitterness.

10

Twenty minutes later I hopped out of the car and wrapped my arms around Brooks's neck. I frickin' loved ecstasy. Brooks twirled me in a circle and guided me into the party, bellowing a greeting as soon as we walked in.

The living room was massive. Painted butter-yellow walls covered by funky art pieces. It'd been cleared of most of the furniture except a makeshift platform for the band and a few chairs on the edges of the room. Everything seemed to hum and wiggle under my gaze. Like there was really life in inanimate objects, but we couldn't see it most of the time. The band stood to the side, surrounded by groupies. There were too many people in the center of the room, waiting for the music to start. I wanted to talk to all of them. They sparkled, and the sway of the collective group made me want to join the mass and dance until my feet hurt. And the smell—sweat, perfume, deodorant, pot, cologne, cigarettes—it was delicious. Ricardo was in the corner, playing a guitar. I beelined toward him and nearly jumped in his lap.

"I can't believe you're here. It's so cool that you're here." I smiled at him and he looked at me funny.

"Thanks."

Brooks slid in next to me and I introduced him to Ricardo.

"He's like the coolest guy. Well, you both are. But Ricardo is this amazing worker and he's so patient with Dennis. And he's pretty good with tools. He's going to college for architecture or something." Bubbles popped inside me and I grinned.

"Do I need to be jealous?" Brooks said, and laughed. I turned and planted a full-mouth kiss on him.

"Jesus," Ricardo said, holding up his hand. "There are children present. Spare me the tonsil hockey."

I giggled and Ricardo rolled his eyes. He shifted his gaze to Brooks. "You gave her something?"

Brooks smiled and shrugged.

I grabbed Ricardo's hands and squeezed. They were so smooth and strong. "Yes. E. It's amazing. Seriously. Amazing."

Ricardo disentangled his hands from mine and pulled himself off the chair before mumbling "This should be interesting" and then walking away with his guitar tucked beneath his arm.

Brooks dropped into the chair and tugged me onto his

lap. I could feel every part of his body pressing against mine. I looked at him and tried to keep my face serious, but it was no use. I grinned.

"I'm still not having sex with you."

"So you said." He put his hand over his heart. "I promise, I won't make unwanted advances toward you."

He was so adorable I wanted to devour him. It was the drugs, but I didn't care. It didn't change anything about how I felt. I straddled a leg on either side of his hips and stared at him. He gripped my thighs and I winced when he grazed the tender cut on my inner thigh. His fingers traced the path of it and he shook his head.

"You were supposed to be done with this," he said.

I bit my lip. "You were at AA."

He lifted me out of the chair and dragged me into a small, dark room filled with coats piled on a couch. "Gannon," he said between little kisses, "repeat after me. I will not cut when Brooks isn't around."

"I will not cut when Brooks isn't around," I whispered.

He kissed me fully then. Hard. And I got too swept up in it. My shirts were off before I knew it. His too. He laid me down on two scratchy coats he pulled from the couch and explored all the parts of me he could reach. My skin tingled everywhere. His fingers were like a trail of liquid fire all over my body. Then I flipped him and did the same to him. I was pressed against him, sucking on his nipple ring, when I heard someone come in the room. Brooks's hand shooed our guest away, and because of the ecstasy I wasn't even bothered by the fact that someone had just seen me with no top, scars, cuts, and all.

Ali took me home. After the marathon make-out session Brooks drank too much and I left him with his head in the toilet and his keys in my pocket. I begged Ricardo to drive him home and then trailed out the door behind Ali, the effects of E finally subsiding. She eyed me for too long without saying a word. I finally turned on her.

"Say it. Whatever you're thinking. Just frickin' say it."

She grinned. "I didn't think you had it in you. I'm sort of proud of you."

I gaped at her. This was my big lecture about hanging around with the wrong guy and doing E? My best friend was kind of worthless.

"I did E."

She giggled. "Yeah. I know. So does everyone. It wasn't hard to figure out. You went from being Eeyore to Tigger in one party. That shit doesn't happen without some serious drugs."

"Someone walked in on me making out with Brooks."

She nodded. "Yeah. Like six different people did. You guys were loud."

I didn't say anything. She stared at me and then returned

her gaze to the road. "Do you wanna tell me about your stomach?"

I swallowed. "Not really."

She maneuvered her car into my driveway. "Well, I think that sucks. Best friends are supposed to tell each other stuff. I told you about Skeevy Dave. What the hell is going on?"

I shook my head. It was one thing to tell Brooks, but I didn't think I could explain it to Ali. Her life was possibly shittier than mine, and she didn't feel the need to carve herself up every time she got overwhelmed. What was I supposed to say?

"Will you at least tell me about Brooks?"

"What do you want to know?" I gave her a tiny smile.

"Have you slept with him?"

"No," I said, and stared at the door of my too-quiet house. My stomach clenched. Something felt wrong.

"Will you tell me when you do?"

I nodded, still watching the house.

"I'm not against it or anything. I'm just not sure you have all the information on him." Her hands skimmed over her holey jeans, scratching the fabric with her chipped nails.

I shook my head. I didn't want to get into a Brooks discussion with Ali, especially since her taste in guys didn't exactly recommend her as the best person to give advice. "Thanks for the ride. I gotta go. I'll talk to you on Monday."

I stepped out of her car and walked too fast to the front

door. It was late, but my house was never this dark. Mom always left the light on for me when I was out. And sometimes Dad stayed up late watching ESPN in the living room. It was the only time he ever got to watch the big TV.

My key shook in my hand as I pressed it into the lock. I stumbled inside and found Mom curled in a heap on the couch under an afghan my grandma had knitted her for her anniversary. Her eyes were red and swollen, and she stared at me hopefully for a second before turning away and wrapping the afghan tighter around herself.

"What's wrong?"

"They've run away."

"What?" I closed the distance to the couch. "When?"

"A few hours ago. After the movie. We told them to get ready for bed. Dad and I were doing the dishes, and when we went to tuck them in, we couldn't find them."

"Why didn't you call me?"

"Because it's not your problem, Amelia. They shouldn't always be your problem."

She looked old and tired. A part of me ached for her. "Did you call the police?"

She nodded. "Dad's out looking with them now."

I sat down and leaned against her, our shoulders touching. I wrapped my arm around her awkwardly. We hadn't touched in forever. The two of us sat on the couch in silence, waiting. I stared at the clock on the cable box and thought about calling Brooks and telling him to come help us look for the boys. But then I remembered he was too wasted to drive, and a big part of me didn't want him to be any more involved in *my* crap salad.

Twenty minutes later Dad walked in with the boys. Alex was asleep on his shoulder. Mom shot from the couch and crowded them, her arms enveloping them, words of worry and gratitude and love spilling from her mouth.

The boys' wide eyes blinked. They didn't explain, just accepted Mom's hugs and stayed huddled together in the front hallway. I rose from the couch and saw a strange look cross Luis's face. He gave me a tiny smile and nod. Oh God. He was a master manipulator. He knew exactly what he was doing. My stomach turned inside out. Without a word I passed them and walked up the steps to my room.

11

I said less than a dozen words during the entire breakfast at the House of Pancakes the next morning. Mom did most of the talking, reminding the boys over and over how she couldn't lose them, they could never run away again. I could barely touch my waffles and had probably had five cups of coffee by the time it was over.

The ecstasy had left me thirsty, but after chugging two full water bottles in the middle of the night, I felt relatively normal.

"So where'd you guys go last night?" I finally asked, because I couldn't stand all Mom's talking anymore.

Luis smiled at me, but before he could say anything, Dad interrupted, "I found them at the park. Can you believe it? They were on the swings." He laughed, but it was nervous and wrong.

I opened my mouth to lay into them about how worried

Mom had been, but I closed it when I saw her face. She knew they'd staged the whole thing. Ran away and returned like prodigal sons. Everyone at the table knew. *Sometimes lying is really the kindest option.*

"I'm going over to Brooks's today." The minute it slipped out of my mouth, I felt the rightness of it. "We're going to watch a movie." He owed me *Fright Night* even if he was hungover.

Mom gave me a genuine smile. "Okay. That sounds like fun. But be home early. School night."

The tiny frown on Dad's forehead disappeared as soon as I turned my attention fully to him. "Yeah. Home before ten." He ruffled my striped hair but pulled his hand away as soon as he realized it was stiff and caked in gel.

I grinned at him and for half a second pretended it was just the three of us at the table. That Dad might invite Brooks over to our house to watch the movie all together. That Mom would cook us butternut squash soup and make me leave the door to my room open when I brought Brooks upstairs. For half a second I pretended they cared.

Then Luis spilled his water and Alex started screaming because his pants got wet and Miguel added salt to Dad's coffee without him noticing. And we were us again. I flipped my phone open in the midst of the chaos and texted Brooks. I hoped he was up and had retrieved his car so that he could come get me.

• • •

An hour and a half later Brooks picked me up from my house and tucked me into his car after a quick handshake introduction with Dad and a few words of bullshit chitchat with Mom. A cigarette was in my mouth before we'd even turned the corner on my block.

"My brothers ran away last night," I said, blowing a ring of smoke out the window.

Brooks laughed. "Clever bastards."

I scoffed.

"Oh, come on, Gannon. Admit it. They're messed up, but it's fun to watch them."

"No. Not when you're in it."

Brooks reached over and pulled on a piece of my hair. "Poor baby."

"Fuck off."

"Yes, please. When?"

The air in the car shifted. My fingernails pressed into my palms, and the silence wrapped around me like tentacles of an octopus. Parts of my body still tingled from Brooks's hands the night before, but the other part got all knotted up at the idea of sleeping with him.

"I've only known you three weeks," I finally said.

He shrugged. "And?"

I stubbed my cigarette out and lit another before answering. "I'm a virgin."

"So?"

"So." I took a long drag. "It's a big deal."

"Aw, Christ, you're not one of those girls, are you?"

"What girls?"

"The ones saving themselves."

I shook my head. "It's not that."

Brooks pulled to the side of the road and scooped me closer to him. "I'm not worthy, then?" He grinned, but I saw a flash of something sad in his eyes.

My free hand slid over his chest and I felt his nipple ring through his shirt. "You might be," I said, and grinned back at him. "Too soon to tell."

I thought he'd accept my brush-off, but suddenly his hand gripped my inner thigh. The cuts flared, scraping against the seam of my pants. A line of blood seeped through the denim. "Is it because of this?"

His hand eased up and I shifted away, stubbing out my cigarette and tucking it back into the box.

"I don't know."

He released a frustrated breath and pulled the car back on to the street. He wanted an answer I couldn't give him. When we were together, my body reacted to him like he was part of my own skin. But it wasn't enough. Something stopped me from letting go with him. Even on E I'd held part of myself back.

"Where are we going?" I asked after too much silence.

"My place. We both need some sleep."

Brooks's house was a tiny green bungalow in desperate need of new stucco. A pile of newspapers littered the porch, and the front door had scuff marks like someone had tried to kick their way in. When we walked inside, I gasped at the number of books stacked everywhere in the house. They were piled on tables and chairs and crammed in bookshelves. I couldn't see any surface not covered in them.

"Foster mom's a reader, huh?"

"Yeah."

"That's cool." I didn't know what else to say. Was I supposed to state the obvious—this house was two months and ten cats away from being a hoarder's palace?

"I'm eighteen in a few months," Brooks said, answering a question I didn't ask. "I'll be out soon."

An older woman in a robe wandered out of the kitchen. She saw me and immediately tightened the robe sash and stood taller.

"Who's this, Michael?" Her gaze narrowed on him, an unspoken reprimand. The gray curls on her head were slightly matted, but she seemed almost regal, standing before us with her arms crossed.

"This is Gannon. Gannon, this is Sue."

"Amelia, actually. Nice to meet you." I stuck out my hand, but she just nodded and looked me over. My hand dropped and I eyed the stairway. How much time did I need to spend with her? I clearly didn't have Brooks's ability to charm moms.

"It's your night to cook dinner," she said, turning to Brooks. "If your friend is staying, you'll need to buy more chicken."

"I'm—" I started.

"She won't be staying," Brooks interrupted. Not that I wanted to, but he didn't have to be rude about it. "We're working on a school project. I'll drive her home before I make dinner."

She nodded and turned back to the kitchen, her robe sash dropping as her feet shuffled along. Maybe not so regal after all.

Brooks grabbed my hand and steered me into a small windowless room at the top of the stairs. He flicked on a light and I surveyed the space. Single futon mattress on the floor with an itchy-looking striped blanket thrown over it. Posters of football players on the walls. Coffee can with cigarette butts next to a pouch of Indian Spirit tobacco and some rolling papers. Black duffel bag stuffed in the corner.

"Football fan?" I asked, settling myself on the mattress.

"No. But I guess the guy before me was."

"No windows?"

He shrugged. "I think this used to be a closet."

I nodded as he sat next to me. He grabbed the rolling papers and started to roll himself a cigarette. I watched in fascination as his hands moved over the paper. The same hands that had moved over me. The same long fingers that had traced all my scars.

He lit the cigarette and handed it to me before rolling a second one. I took a long drag and then coughed.

"Not exactly filtered menthols," he said with a laugh.

I took a smaller drag and felt the buzz of the unfiltered cigarette swirl around my head. Brooks lit his cigarette and the two of us sat without saying anything, tapping ashes into the coffee can. I couldn't tell if he was angry about the whole sex thing. He seemed like the same unfazed Brooks, but I was beginning to wonder how much of that was show.

Before I could ask, the door to his room banged open and a pale guy with a shaved head and no shirt stood in the doorway. He glanced at Brooks and then moved his gaze to me, staring so long my skin began to crawl. I shifted back on the futon.

Brooks placed his hand on my knee. "Gannon, this is Ray. Ray, this is Gannon."

Ray's skin hung off his bones and his eyes had deep purple circles beneath them. The smell coming off him made me want to bury my face in Brooks's T-shirt.

After a final appraisal of me, his gaze zeroed in on Brooks. "I need you to talk to Kenji for me."

Brooks drew on his cigarette and shook his head. "Talk to him yourself."

"I can't. I owe him money. You got to get him to loan me something."

Brooks scoffed. "Loan you something? Are you planning on giving it back?"

"Fuck you. Just talk to him, will you?"

Brooks stubbed out his cigarette. "No. That shit's between you and Kenji. I did you a favor once, but I'm not about to make a habit of it."

"I need this." Ray's face had the same desperate look I'd seen on the meth heads at the Punkin' Donuts. I shifted closer to Brooks.

"Tough shit. This isn't my problem," Brooks said.

Ray glared daggers at the two of us. "I won't forget this, brother. You better watch your back." He snatched the handle of the door and slammed it so hard I heard Sue's voice yell upstairs.

"He's your brother?" I asked, dropping my cigarette into the coffee can.

"No. He's one of the other guys who lives here. I should have known better than to help him out in the first place. Junkies are always the same."

How much experience did Brooks have with junkies? Sometimes the reality of his life seemed so far away from my own pathetic existence.

"Are you worried?"

"Not really," he said, shrugging. "Strung-out junkies are loud and clumsy, and mostly forget every threat they make."

He pulled me into the nest of itchy blanket and wrapped his arms around me. He was quiet for so long I thought he'd fallen asleep, but then he kissed the top of my head.

"You're the only one who means anything to me. And I'm not mad about the sex thing," he whispered. "But when you decide, I want your first time to be with me."

"I'm not exactly interviewing other candidates," I said, nestling closer to him.

"You better not be." He plucked at my hair. "This," he said, sliding his hands over me. "This belongs to me."

I smacked him. "Such a caveman. You're not exactly sweeping me off my feet here."

He drew his fingers along the back of my neck. "Yes, I am."

I didn't answer him. His possessiveness scared me as much as it drew me in. His arms tightened, and even though part of me was terrified of what he was becoming to me, I couldn't make myself pull away. I melted into him, dropping into a deep, dreamless sleep.

12

Dealing with some shit. Be back in a month. Wait for me.

I searched the hallways of school the morning he texted me. After I'd sent him back a dozen text responses, questions, pleas. Of course he wasn't at school; he'd said as much. I wanted to ask his friends where he was, but it occurred to me I'd never seen Brooks with the same group of people. Everyone knew of him, but no one knew anything about him. All day I itched with loneliness and the stifling weight of not right.

Be back in a month.

Three days in and I felt like I could barely breathe. Mom didn't ask anything when I got home that afternoon. Just like she hadn't the day before, or the one before that. Like she didn't even recognize something was off. She needed help getting Luis to soccer and Alex to the eye doctor. I sat in the grass, watching Luis mess around and ignore the soccer coach while I waited for Mom to come back. My fingers plucked at pieces of grass, weaving them together, ripping them apart. And I tried to inhale through the pain of wanting Brooks. Too much.

Dealing with some shit.

I reread Brooks's text for the hundredth time. I'd taken to texting him every night, but heard nothing from him. Ten days felt like a thousand. I stared at my TV, watching movies I'd seen and used to love. They were dots on a screen now. Nothing but added minutes to help me pass through the tunnel of not seeing Brooks.

Wait for me.

Nineteen days into the month I started asking everyone if they knew where he was, even people I'd never spoken to in my life, but no one had a clue. They all offered ridiculous explanations that I hoped weren't true.

"The brother of the guy he killed put a hit on him."

"He's been busted for a gay porn ring."

"He OD'd and is in a coma."

I stumbled through each day, checking my phone incessantly. Each patch of blue I glimpsed made my heart thunk in my chest. *Wait for me.* Every moment of every day was filled with wait. My brain was fuzzy and I spent too much time recounting the hours I'd spent with Brooks, always wondering, worrying. I carefully put my hoops in my ears every morning and pretended it didn't matter. And I hated so much that it did.

Twenty-three days in, I went to his house. Sue wouldn't answer any of my questions when I pounded on her screen door demanding to know where he was.

She pursed her lips at me and said, "He woulda told you if he wanted you to know where he went."

"But what if—"

She slammed the door in my face and wouldn't open it again.

I imagined the worst. It was Brooks, after all. At home I smoked out of my window and spent too many nights looking at my razors, but I never used them. My fingers played over them again and again. On the twenty-fifth night I got close enough to make a tiny slice on my thumb, but I pulled back. The adrenaline rush was still there, but so much anxiety swirled around it that it didn't feel like the same kind of high. The worry over what Brooks would say if he found new cuts on me overrode my addiction. Somehow the cutting didn't seem worth it. A part of me was aware enough to know I was replacing one thing for another, but it didn't matter. Not to the need inside me.

So I waited for him and chided myself for having fallen hard enough to miss him. It was the touching. I missed touch. His touch.

Ali picked me up from work on the twenty-seventh day. "So it doesn't look like he's coming back, huh?"

I blew a smoke ring at her. "Not one to mince words, are you?"

"I told you I'd heard shit about him."

I shut my eyes and leaned against the window. "I don't want to talk about him."

The month was almost up. I could wait. I could hold out a few days more. Alone.

"I'm just saying, it's stupid to pine away for a guy who isn't exactly reliable."

"I said I didn't want to talk about him."

I shut my eyes and ignored the voice in the back of my head wondering if he was just stringing me along. If it would be more than a month. If he'd taken off for good.

"Okay, fine," Ali said. "We won't talk about him. You wanna go to Dark Alley with me? Jace is working. He loves when I visit. He calls it the merging of his two alleys."

I snorted. This Jace was such a winner. The only time I'd met him, he'd had his tongue in Ali's mouth the second we walked into the store and barely acknowledged me. Who the hell was I to talk, though?

"No." I stubbed out my cigarette. "Not today. I've got stuff to do."

She looked at me sideways, her eyes zeroing in on my stomach. I crossed my arms and stared back at her. She shook her head and sighed.

"You should hang out with us. I talk about you all the time."

I nodded. "Soon."

"When?"

"I don't know. Soon."

"Later this week, then," she said, and pulled into my driveway.

"Sure. Fine." Later this week, when Brooks would be back.

My house was mass chaos when I entered. Again. The running-away incident had been leveraged to its maximum benefit and now Mom was back to shrieking at my brothers. Alex and Miguel had tied Luis to a kitchen chair and were dousing him with shaving cream as Mom tried to unknot his wrists.

"Stop it, boys. Enough! I said *stop*."

Luis wiggled and winked at his brothers. When she finally loosened the knot, he turned to her and batted his eyes. His body was covered in shaving cream, but still he said in a reasonable voice, "It was just a game, Mom."

She pointed the boys to the back door and they saluted her, then marched out, giggling. She leaned down and mopped up some of the shaving cream before sitting down and putting her head in her hands.

"You okay?" I asked.

"Fine," she said. "You?"

"Yep."

"Where's Michael been?"

I knelt and helped her wipe up the rest of the shaving cream. "Don't know."

She touched my forearm and then pulled her hand back. "Well, don't worry about it. Boyfriends come and go. Another one will pop up, I'm sure."

Sometimes lying is really the kindest option.

"I'm sure." I dropped the paper towels into the trash and headed up to my room for another horror-movie marathon. I ignored my homework and stayed up too late thinking about Brooks.

Thirty-five days. Thirty-five fucking days. No Brooks. *Be back in a month* was a cruel joke. I deleted his text and stopped feeling anything at all.

Dennis had concocted a huge after-Thanksgiving sale to get rid of extra inventory. He wanted me to build wooden birdhouses to mark the sale aisles. It was the stupidest idea I'd ever heard, but he threatened to fire me if I didn't do it and I thought he might be serious.

"Why don't you just put sale signs over these aisles?"

"Shut it," Dennis barked at me.

"I'm just saying, a bunch of birdhouses isn't gonna let people know they can take fifty percent off of all the merchandise."

"Quit your bitching. You've been in a surly mood this past month and you need to snap out of it."

I gaped at him. Was I that obvious? "No, I haven't."

Dennis shook his head and exchanged a look with Ricardo. "Yes, you have. Now just finish putting your tools away and get your head in the game or I'm dropping you."

I wasn't the only surly one. Dennis had been on his period ever since Brooks had shown up drunk that day.

"You're not dropping me. No one else can work the Skilsaw."

"Ricardo can. And working the Skilsaw isn't a requirement of the job."

"It is if you have to build bullshit birdhouses," I mumbled.

Dennis's nostrils flared. "No more discussion. Tools away and you better be back here this weekend to work the sale."

I opened my mouth to argue more, but Dennis held up his hand. When the hand came up, I knew Dennis was really pissed. I shut my mouth and moved to the storage garage. What did I care anyway? I had nowhere else to be.

The lights flickered as I stood surveying the piles of wood and tools littered along the floor. I sat down and started collecting nails, putting them into the tiny, labeled boxes Dennis housed them in. The door to the storage garage creaked open and my head whipped up.

Brooks. Heat I hadn't felt in days surged into my body. My hands trembled and I clenched them into fists.

"Where the hell have you been?"

He took a tentative step toward me. "Rehab."

"Really?" My hands unclenched and my eyes scanned his body as I got to my feet. He'd gotten thinner, and something about his face looked not quite right.

"Yeah. Sue found some E in my duffel and sort of over-reacted. I think fucking Ray tipped her off about it. She told me I needed to pull my shit together and get clean if I wanted to stay with her."

He moved closer to me, and his hand reached out to trace the hoops in my ear. I shut my eyes for a second and allowed his long fingers to figure-eight around the silver before I shook him off.

"You could've called me or returned my texts. It's been thirty-five days. Longer than a month." My breath came in short bursts, squeezed from the hole in my throat that had been shrinking since the moment he left.

His fingers moved to the now completely faded hickey on my neck. He circled it, his thumb brushing over the smoothness as he stared at me, took all of me in with his too-keen eyes. Butterflies fluttered around my stomach. Then he dropped his mouth to my pale skin and sucked hard. My insides coiled; the butterflies stilled. I released a long shaky breath.

"They took my cell, and it wasn't the kind of rehab where you get to make a bunch of phone calls," he said, nipping me with his teeth.

"Are you going to apologize?" I grabbed at my last vestiges of logic and pushed him off my neck.

"I don't do apologies," he said, and his hands circled my waist before he plunged his mouth onto mine. His tongue traced my bottom lip, pressing me to open.

Part of me wanted to push him away. Drop him before he bailed on me all over again. Make him beg for my forgiveness. But seeing him in front of me, practically vibrating with want, made everything fall out of my head. It was like an IV of ecstasy pumped directly into my heart.

I clung to his neck. His hands slid beneath the back of my shirt, moving up and down my spine. I raked my fingers through his hair and opened my mouth wider. My entire body trembled with how much I'd missed him.

He pulled away for a second, dropping kisses along my jaw before whispering, "Does the door lock?"

I nodded, drawing in a quick breath. Dennis had installed a lock on the inside of the door a month after he realized how much time I spent alone working there.

Brooks released me and went to shut and lock the door.

"Let me see you," he said, stepping toward me and lifting me onto Dennis's worktable. He moved his hands to the bottom of my shirt.

I stilled for a second and then helped him pull my shirt off. His hands shook a little when he lifted off the next layer, my thin tank top.

"You're shaking."

He grinned at me. "Anticipation."

The lump in my throat got bigger. "Really?"

His hands moved over my stomach, sliding over old scars. "Really. It's been a long thirty-five days." His warm breath tickled my neck and his hands dropped to the belt loops on the hips of my jeans. "I want to see *all* of you."

His fingers moved to the button on my fly and I dropped my hands on top of his for a second. I stared into his dark eyes, trying to figure out all the emotions held in them. Trying to figure out what I wanted.

"Please," he whispered.

One word and I was undone. I released my hands, slipped off the worktable, and kicked off my shoes. He knelt and peeled off my jeans. His eyes scanned my entire body.

"Gorgeous." He breathed into my stomach, fingers continuing to trace the pattern of my scars. His hands dropped down to my legs. He smiled. "And unmarked."

"I told you I wouldn't cut," I whispered, then reached for

him, dropping to the ground. I kissed him, teasing his mouth open and trying to push all my overwhelming feelings into him. But my body remained tense, unwilling to allow the emotional assault to break through. I kissed Brooks harder and dug my fingers into his neck.

He pulled away from me, searching my face. "What's wrong?"

"N-nothing," I stuttered.

"Yes, something is. What do you want?"

"I need, I need . . ." I looked away. I couldn't grab hold of my racing thoughts. It was too much, and the familiar shut-down teased the edges of my consciousness.

Brooks reached past me to the worktable. He snatched a black object and held it behind him.

"Tell me what you want," he said again.

I shivered. The cold cement floor had too many points of contact with my bare skin. I even felt it through my thin under-wear. Brooks hauled himself up and grabbed a painting tarp with his free hand. He dropped it next to me and spread it out with his feet before shifting me onto it.

"Anything. I'll give you anything. Just tell me what you want."

Goose bumps formed on my arms and legs, but I knew they weren't from the cold. "It's too much. Seeing you. It's too much. It's been too long. I can't do this. I need—"

My throat closed up. I couldn't say it. I curled into a ball and reached for my shirt. Brooks stopped me. He moved his hand from behind his back and revealed a utility knife. My body unwound from the inside out.

"This?" he said, sliding the blade out of its casing.

I looked away from him and nodded.

"Look at me," he commanded. "Gannon. Look at me right now."

I brushed away the tears in the corners of my eyes and met his gaze. His fingers traced a path along my face. He slid the knife back into its black shell.

"If we do this," he said in a low voice, "I need you to tell me when to stop. Do you understand?"

I nodded.

"Say it."

"I understand," I whispered. "I'll tell you when to stop."

He pulled his shirt off and inched closer to me, kneeling next to my legs. The blade of the utility knife slid out and my heart thumped faster. I reached to touch his nipple ring and he moved his mouth to my stomach. He licked a small circle around my belly button and then replaced his tongue with the blade.

The first cut barely grazed me, but I moaned. It'd been too long since I'd cut. Brooks dug the tip a little deeper and a hiss escaped my mouth. He pulled back.

"It's okay," I said, drawing him back in. I rolled over and guided his hand to the back of my thighs. "Here. Cut here."

My stomach and chest pressed against the coarse paint tarp, but I didn't even notice because he was suddenly behind me, his legs straddling my waist, slicing. It was too much. Too deep. But I couldn't say the word. Emotions poured out of me, layer upon layer spilling onto the floor.

"Christ," he whispered. But then he made another cut next to the first.

Agony. Blood dripped down the back of my leg in sticky lines and tears pricked my eyes.

"One more," I said, half command, half plea.

The knife dropped from his hand and he snatched his shirt and pressed it to my bleeding thigh. "No. We're done. I shouldn't have—"

I rolled over and sat up. I grabbed the shirt from him and tied it around my thigh in a makeshift tourniquet. "Don't. You will *not* start in with the regrets. I asked you to do this."

He was silent. He pushed his hair out of his face and stared at me. "Is it better, then?"

I slipped into his lap and kissed him with everything I had. The cut on my stomach stung when it touched his body, my thigh burned, but none of it mattered. I teased the buckle on his belt and then helped him take off his pants. He fumbled with his wallet and pulled out a condom. We rolled back onto the tarp, and for the first time in forever I felt free. I shifted back and circled my fingers in patterns across his chest. He smiled his boyish grin at me.

"My turn."

I lifted myself up, wincing as the shirt tourniquet rode up my leg. "Your turn for what?"

"My turn to get what I want."

He pulled me back onto him and then there was nothing between us but skin and hands and mouths and tongues and blood and want.

13

I hobbled through my front door hours later. My body felt like it had been assaulted by a bear. Everything ached and I was grinning like an asshole. I smelled like sex and sweat and blood and Brooks.

"What happened to you?" Mom asked as soon as I walked in the door.

"Nothing. Why?"

"You're limping." She squinted her eyes at me.

"I had to put away all the tools. I banged the back of my leg on Dennis's tool shelf."

She pursed her lips. "Let me see." She stepped toward me, but I waved my hands and retreated.

"I'm fine. It's a little bruise. I'm just tired from work."

Before she could say anything else, I bolted up the stairs,

taking them two at a time even though pain ripped through me. My pants were covered with blood by the time I got to my room. I stepped into the bathroom and locked the door behind me. I snatched hydrogen peroxide and large bandages from the medicine cabinet. Thank God for my constantly injured, destructive brothers.

The peroxide stung when I blotted it on, and more blood dripped from my leg before I could place the bandage. I ended up scrubbing drops of red off the oatmeal-colored tile, then balling everything into my jeans and sneaking into my room.

I lay in the dark, my hands roving over the new marks on my body. I shut my eyes and remembered the look on Brooks's face when he slid inside me. He'd whispered sweet words in my ear so the pain wouldn't be so bad. It hurt, but it didn't matter. Every part of me had been branded as his.

I stood staring at the numbers on my combination lock for too long. My phone pinged in my pocket.

Ali: *I need to talk to you.*

I ignored her text and spun the lock again. I couldn't gather my thoughts. They all revolved around Brooks. Then he was behind me. Kissing my neck as if he'd heard me thinking about him, wanting him, needing him.

"I missed you."

I snorted. "You saw me less than twenty-four hours ago."

"Too long." He pulled at my shirt and kissed my collarbone. "I have something for you," he said.

"Yeah?"

"Yeah. But you'll have to wait for it until after school."

I swatted him. "Tease."

He licked his lips and kissed my cheek. "Yes. Yes, I am."

"I have to finish cleaning up the storage garage. Dennis is pissed. He called this morning and read me the riot act. Said my ass better be there this afternoon or he'd fire me for real." I smiled. "Also, he wanted to know where his paint tarp went."

Brooks chuckled. "Did he check the Dumpster?"

I eased my books into my bag and slammed my locker shut. Brooks kissed me and grabbed my bag. "What're you doing?"

"Walking you to class."

I stared at him sideways. "That's sort of chivalrous."

He grinned. "Yeah, well, I told you I missed you." He ducked his head, but not before I caught a tiny blush on his cheeks.

I reached out and grabbed his hand. So not my style, but I couldn't help it. "Me too. But my class is right here." I pointed to the room in front of us.

"Oh. Okay. Well, meet me before you have to go help

Dennis." He slung my bag over my shoulder. "I promise it'll just be for a few minutes."

I bit my lip then nodded. "Okay. In back of the store at four o'clock."

He traced the hoops on my ear and then walked away whistling. I wanted to follow him, stay with him, drown in him. But the still-sane part of me turned toward class and steeled myself against my too-real feelings.

My English teacher asked me to come by after school to discuss my unwillingness to live up to my potential. She blathered on about seeing something special in my writing and wanting me to explore it, while I stared at the clock and occasionally nodded at her. My teachers had been discussing my lack of academic effort since I'd started high school. I wasn't a horrible student. I wasn't a great student. I was a student who got by. Putting forth a lot of effort in school was stupid. I was bound for community college at best. My parents had raided my college fund to adopt the boys, and with all the therapy they hadn't been able to replace any of the money. Mom had looked guilty when she'd told me, but Dad had said he'd managed college without funds from his parents and it was unrealistic for schools to expect generous donations from parents.

"Amelia, I'm saying that you have a gift. Maybe you could

put it to good use," Mrs. Simone said for the third time.

"Thanks," I said, hoping unresponsiveness would get me out of this and back to Brooks.

"Have you ever considered the literary magazine?"

I choked on a laugh. "Umm . . . I don't think so. I'm not really a joiner."

Her flaky lipsticked lips dropped into a frown. "It'd look good on your college applications. You should start thinking about your future."

I slid my hand underneath my thigh and pressed lightly. A bite of pain and so much relief. "Yep. I should. Well, thanks for the advice. I gotta go."

She shook her head and passed me my paper. "You're a good writer. Don't give up on it."

I nodded and escaped her classroom, tossing the paper in the trash on my way out of school, moving faster than my leg really wanted me to so I could get back to Brooks.

He was leaning against the brick wall of the store when I walked up.

"Sorry."

He shrugged. "Thought maybe you weren't coming." His voice quivered a little and my stomach flooded in warmth.

"Were you worried?"

He looked at his boots. "I just got you back."

My feet inched closer to him without me even being fully aware of it. He was like a magnet. "I just got *you* back."

He grinned at me. "Yes. Yes, you did. So are you ready for my surprise?"

I leaned in and inhaled his scent. Indian Spirit cigarettes and sweat and deodorant and boy. "Yes," I breathed.

He pulled me around the corner behind the Dumpster. I dropped my bag and wrapped my arms around his neck, kissing a path down his jaw. He uncoiled my arms and stepped back from me to lift his shirt up, tossing it to the ground like he was dropping a surrender flag. My breath caught.

At first I thought he'd taken a razor blade to his chest, but as I stepped closer, I saw it was a bright red tattoo designed to give the impression of knife scratches. It was a misshapen heart with stitches across it. Tiny red straight pins speared the heart in six places across the top. The heads of the pins were circles with letters in them: *GANNON*.

"What'd you do?" I reached out to touch him and he hissed.

"Easy. It's healing. I need to put some more ointment on it."

My mouth opened and closed. "Why did you do this?"

He closed the distance between us and slid his hand under my shirt. His fingers moved over the cuts around my belly button. The cuts he'd made. "I'd do anything for you."

I couldn't speak. Couldn't breathe. Everything between us was so intense. My fingers moved gently to the tattoo. "I can't believe you did this. I've never had anyone do something so crazy for me."

He lifted me up and slid his hand to the back of my bandaged thigh. "Anything. Do you understand? I'd do anything. I'm yours. Completely."

I kissed him, wrapping myself around him as tightly as I could. Not wanting to escape. He dug his fingers into my thigh. I cried out in pain but held his hand there. I started to pull off my own shirt when there was a loud thump on the Dumpster. Dennis stood in front of us with his hands on his hips.

"Gannon. Say good-bye to your Smurf and get your ass in the garage right now."

Brooks grinned, reached for his shirt, and tugged it back on. "I'll see you later, sweetheart."

I smiled at him and dutifully followed Dennis toward the storage garage. I glanced back at Brooks and he winked at me.

Dennis mumbled the entire time he messed with the padlocks. When he finally got the garage open, he pointed me to the pile of tools and huffed as he moved to the scrap-wood corner. After twenty minutes of flinging pieces of wood around, he joined me on the ground, separating nails.

"I'm not sure the Smurf is good for you."

"What?"

"The Blue Man. The boy with the piercings and the tattoo.

I'm not sure this is a good choice for you." He released a long breath.

"And you can weigh in on this, why?"

"Gannon. You're my employee and I'd like to think a friend. I probably know you better than your own parents. I know kids these days dress differently and mark their bodies in all manner of ways, but this is more than that."

Yes, it was. But I wasn't about to share that with Dennis.

"You're flaking out on me, kid," he continued. "And I've got a hundred dollars that says he's the reason."

"I'm not flaking out on you." It was a hollow protest and we both knew it.

"Aw, Christ, Gannon, I thought you were smarter than to get reeled in by some bad boy with a nipple ring."

"You saw that?"

"Of course I saw it," he grumbled. "He wasn't wearing a shirt. And the carved-up heart with your name on it? Where did you find this kid?"

"He found me."

Dennis barked out a short laugh. "Of course he did. You're like a golden ticket to someone like him."

"That's not true."

"Yes it is. That kid's a loser, and you're just the kind of person who'll stroke his ego enough he'll think he's worth something."

I sucked in a breath. "That's cruel."

Dennis shrugged. "Maybe. But it's true. You're better than this one, and if I were you, I'd think long and hard about getting involved with a boy who brands your name on his body just because you opened your legs for him."

His words ripped through me. This was my boss, Dennis? My friend? "Fuck off, Dennis. You're not my dad."

He shook his head at me. "Sometimes I wish I was," he mumbled.

My hands trembled as I put the rest of the tools away. I slipped away as soon as I could, not even nodding good-bye to Dennis.

I wanted Brooks. Needed him. And then he was there. Sitting on his car in the Punkin' parking lot, smoking a cigarette, waiting for me. The relief was immediate. Powerful. Addictive. Better than anything I'd ever felt before.

14

"I think we should do E again." I was wrapped in a blanket in the back of Brooks's car, staring at the scuff marks on the vinyl seat.

He shifted me on top of him and played with the ends of my hair. "Really?"

"Yeah. I liked it."

He grinned and cupped my chin. "Yeah. I thought you might. Not really a good idea, though."

"Are you worried about Sue?"

He shook his head. "Not so much. But I'm worried about you. E can be really addictive. I don't think you should be exposed to too many things that are addicting."

I lifted my head. "Why not?"

He chuckled. "Because then you'll fall. It's in your nature. You're a bit compulsive."

I whacked him. "Go to hell. I am not."

He slid his hand down to the back of my thigh. He peeled the bandage off and touched the deep cut lines. "Yes, sweetheart. You are."

"What about you, then?" I pouted.

"Not so much, usually." He pressed the bandage back in place.

"Usually?" I quirked an eyebrow at him.

"With you it's a bit different. I've never wanted anything as much as you before."

My breath caught in a hiccup of happiness and desire. "And you have me."

"Not quite," he whispered into my hair. "But I will."

I'd given him so much. Part of me didn't get why he wouldn't think I was his, but the other part of me knew he was sort of right. I rested my chin on my hands.

"How much more can I give you?"

"How much money do you have saved up?" He grinned and wagged his eyebrows.

"Are you serious?"

"Sort of."

A wrinkle formed in my brow. "I don't know. Most of my paychecks for the past two years. But I'm not lending you money."

"I don't want you to."

"Then what does it matter how much I've got?"

He ran his fingers through my hair. "Run away with me."

I blinked. "What?"

"I'll be eighteen soon. And out of the system. I can do whatever I want. Your birthday is first. You'll be legal. Leave town with me."

"What about school?"

"I probably won't pass. I've missed too much. I can get my GED. So can you."

A lead weight rested in the bottom of my stomach. "Does Sue want you to leave?"

"Probably. I don't know. I haven't really asked her."

I hooked my finger into his nipple ring. "Why do you want to take off?"

He stared at me for too long, his fingers moving over the contours of my face. "So my dad can't find me."

I lifted myself from him. "I thought you hadn't seen him in a long time."

"I haven't," he said, pulling me back down. "But the last time I did, he told me he'd be back for me, my ass belonged to him."

"What? What does that mean?"

He released a sigh. "I assume you've heard about my stint in juvie?"

I pursed my lips.

144

He nodded. "Thought so. Well, it wasn't very long because I was pretty young, but it had to do with my dad."

I laced my fingers through his and squeezed. He squeezed back and my heart thumped.

"I got sent there for stealing a car, driving under the influence."

"Really?" Of all the things Brooks might have done, I hadn't expected that.

"I got sick of all my dad's shit, so one night I broke into his liquor cabinet, then decided to steal his car and take off. He freaked out. Called the cops. I ended up in this police chase and I really had no clue how to drive so I crashed the car. Also I was pretty wasted and there was an open bottle in the car. Frickin' schnapps of all things. The prosecutor was an asshole and my defense attorney sort of phoned it in. Plus, the judge was this old codger who decided to make an example of me even though I was young. The last time Dad saw me, I was being taken away by the cops, and he screamed that he'd kill me for what I did."

"He'd kill you?"

"Yeah. Very fatherly, I know." He shrugged, but I could feel the pain rolling off him in waves. "He really loved that car and I totaled it."

"He put his own son in juvie? Over a car?"

Brooks nodded. The younger version of himself lay beside

me, all anger and hurt and resentment and loneliness. I ached to take it all away from him.

"What was the shit you'd gotten sick of?"

Brooks lifted me off him and turned his back toward me. "This."

I flinched. I'd never get used to the sight of those scars. I wasn't surprised they'd come from his dad; he'd as much as told me without saying the words. But still I could barely wrap my head around it. His own father. My hands moved over the edges of them, tracing the smoothness and slight dents in the skin.

"They put me in the foster system after juvie because they'd seen all the marks and I told them Dad had made them. When they investigated him, he was drunk and got pissed at the case-worker and took a swing at her. That was sort of the nail in the coffin. But I've never doubted he wants to kill me. I'm always watching my back, waiting for him to come after me. I know sometimes it seems like I have a death wish, but I'm not about to go down at the hands of my messed-up old man."

I leaned forward and kissed each mark on his back, letting him feel the tears on my cheek.

"Run away with me," he said, and his voice cracked.

"I don't know," I whispered. "I have to think about it."

The silence in the car cocooned us. Small goose bumps formed on his skin and I tugged the blanket tighter around him. Thoughts darted through my brain, unwilling to land long enough for me to absorb what they all meant. *Stolen car. Juvie. Scars. Run away. Run away. Run away.*

He turned back to me and held my cheeks, brushing away the tears. "I don't have you yet, but I will."

"Do I have you?"

He curled a lock of my zebra hair around his finger and tugged. "Sweetheart. You've had me since the first time I caught you with a menthol."

I grinned and blinked the last of my tears away. "Minty fresh breath."

He chuckled and rolled me underneath him. "Yes. Minty fresh breath," he said before diving into my mouth.

At home I walked in on an argument. A horrible one. I had no idea where my brothers were, but my parents were in the midst of a fierce screaming match the likes of which I'd never heard.

"You can't control me like that. I'm not responsible for your decisions—" Dad's voice cut off when he saw me.

Mom had been crying. Again.

"Where are the boys?"

"Playing with Tim's puppy." Mom's lip quivered.

I opened my mouth to spout about what an absolutely terrible idea that was, but Dad shook his head at me. "You should go keep an eye on them."

I wasn't even out the door before I heard Dad say, "I can't live like this anymore."

My brothers were surprisingly composed around the dog. It was a golden retriever and licked anyone who came near it. The boys couldn't get enough. Alex giggled when the dog jumped on him and slurped his ear. Tim watched with narrowed eyes from the side, but didn't say anything.

"Hey," I said, dropping next to Luis. I smiled at Tim, but he crossed his arms. Too knowing for a little kid. My brothers' sphere of influence had spilled over the edges. Poor Tim.

The weather was cold and I expected snow soon, but the boys were dressed in light coats and seemed oblivious to the oncoming winter.

"Mom and Dad are fighting," Luis said.

I nodded.

"It's about us," he continued.

I shrugged. "Hard to say."

"It is. Dad wants to give us back."

"No, he doesn't."

"I'm not going," he grumbled as if he didn't hear me. "I'll run away before they send me back to Guatemala City."

"I thought you wanted out of this shithole." I nudged him with my knee, trying to erase the wrinkle between his brows.

"Not to go back to an even worse one," he said, all serious face, too old and too jaded for his years.

"He doesn't want to give you back."

"He'll leave, then," Luis said. I glanced at Miguel, who'd been listening to our whole conversation. He shrugged at me.

I wanted to argue, assure them, tell them something that was true. But I had nothing. Dad had mentally checked out over the past year, and nothing Mom did seemed to change how absent he was.

"Amelia," Dad called from the back door of our house.

"Be right back," I whispered, and pretended not to see Miguel reach his hand to Luis's and squeeze hard.

My feet felt weighed down by bricks as I made my way back to where he stood. Was the shitstorm between my parents about to break?

I followed him into the kitchen and crossed my arms, leaning against the sink.

"Your mother and I need a weekend away," Dad said, and my eyes widened.

"What about the boys?"

"It's actually only for one night. Two full days, but only one night." Mom's hands fluttered around her, plucking at her sweater, her buttons, her hair, unable to land on anything.

"Who's going to take care of them?" My voice cracked a bit. I knew how Luis would see this. My parents hadn't been away from them since they got to the States. Mom feared they'd view any kind of departure as abandonment. They might not have when they were younger, but they definitely would now.

"We thought you could," Dad said. "We trust you, and we think the boys will take it better if they aren't left with a stranger."

My heart beat too fast. "I'm not sure that's a good idea."

Mom's eyes had a hint of panic in them, but she stepped toward me and squeezed my shoulder. "Of course it is. You're very responsible. The boys will be in school the Friday we leave, so really it's just Friday night and Saturday that you need to keep an eye on them. We'll be home by Saturday night." She peeked at Dad. "Early."

"I'm seventeen. Even if I am their sister, it's a little much." I wanted to argue that I had work, but I wasn't going back to the store after Dennis's comment about me spreading my legs. Ricardo had texted me four times when I was with Brooks, begging me to come help set up for the sale, but the memory of Dennis's venomous words made walking into Standard feel impossible.

Dad coughed. "Yes, well, we've contacted the Wilsons and they've agreed to keep an eye on the place and help you out if you need it."

It wasn't much, but at least it was a lifeline.

"We trust you, Amelia. And your father and I need some time alone together." Mom gave me a hemorrhoid smile and I thought I might barf. They were going to guilt me into it? I hated them so much.

"I want to be paid." Brooks's plea to run away with him circled around my head. How much hardware money did I have saved? Maybe eighteen hundred dollars? How long would it last us? And did Brooks have any money?

Mom blinked at me, but Dad sighed. "Yes. Of course we'll pay you. We can figure something out."

"When are you planning on leaving?"

"We're talking about next weekend," Dad answered. "We've got Thanksgiving, and know you're working the sale this weekend." I wasn't, of course. But I wasn't about to tell my parents that.

"So next weekend I'm watching the boys for two whole days and you're disappearing?"

Mom nodded grimly. I bit the inside of my cheek and thought about Brooks. I'd spent thirty-five days without him. I hated that I was going to have to add two more. Although if I agreed to run away with him, two days was really nothing in the scheme of the rest of our lives. I released a breath. "You better go tell the boys."

I walked up the stairs and slipped my phone out of my bag.

Gannon: *No fun 4 me next weekend. My parents are out. I'm watching the boys.*

Brooks pinged back right away.

Brooks: *That sounds like LOTS of fun.*

Gannon: *Haha. For you maybe.*

Brooks: *Where are your parents going?*

Gannon: *Away.*

Brooks: *Sounds promising. For how long?*

Gannon: *Friday and Saturday.*

Brooks: *Then we have a plan.* ☺

I blinked at my phone. He couldn't be serious.

Gannon: *You don't think I'll leave my brothers, do you?*

Brooks: *Of course not. But they'll love me. Not to worry.*

Gannon: *You're gonna help me babysit?*

Brooks: *I'm not going to watch those little criminals w/o you*

Gannon: *You're ridiculous. Don't you have better things to do?*

Brooks: *There's nothing better to do than you. xx*

My face flushed. A twinge of guilt tapped at my conscience.
Mom and Dad would never agree to Brooks helping me watch
the boys. I batted the guilt away. They were sucker punching
me into two days with three spawn of the devil; I should be
allowed reinforcements.

Gannon: *Pervert. :P*

I hit end on my phone and pulled my razors from under
my bed. My fingers moved over them, the pad of my thumb
rubbing over the sharp edges. Then, before I could change
my mind, I raced into the hallway and grabbed a bag of craft
supplies out of the closet. I dumped all of Mom's materials on
my carpet floor and grinned like an idiot. *Two days. Two days.
Two days. With Brooks.* It echoed like a mantra in my head.

15

Ali texted me again at lunch the next day.

Ali: *Call me. Now.*

Crap. I'd forgotten about her. She picked up on the first ring.

"Where the hell have you been?"

"Uh, school, where are you?"

She released a deep breath. "Well, Gannon, if you'd answered my texts, you'd know I'm currently in my bedroom after the police paid my mom a visit two days ago."

"What?"

"Yeah. I guess the locker room flooding stunt caused several thousand dollars in damages, and they've made a deal that if I pay full restitution, charges will be dropped. Otherwise I'll be charged with destruction of school property and I'll be doing community service until I'm eighty."

My bag dropped to the floor. I sat down beside it. "Christ, Ali, that sucks. What are you gonna do?"

"Well, Skeevy Dave has offered to loan me the money in exchange for my 'help' with some jobs around his house."

I inhaled deeply. "I don't think that's a good idea, Al."

"Do you have anything better? Do you have money to give me?"

My stomach clenched. I did. Ali knew I did. *Run away with me.* Brooks flashed into my mind. What would he say if I gave all my money to Ali? What would Ali say if I told her I couldn't?

The silence drew out between us. Too long. I opened my mouth but my "yes" refused to pry itself from my lips. Excuses bounced around my brain. My lifeline frayed, unraveled piece by piece, and still I said nothing.

"Forget it, Gannon. I'll figure it out. Have a good Thanksgiving."

"Ali, wait—"

She clicked off. I tried calling her back. Texting her. Nothing. I knew I should give her the money. Skeevy Dave was a bad option. But too many parts of me rebelled at the idea. Everything I'd made in the last few years had been to get out of my crappy house. Could I really give it all up?

The Thanksgiving weekend passed in a haze of Indian Spirit cigarettes and Brooks. Holed up in his room beneath his scratchy

154

striped blanket, lost in each other for hours. I should've gone to see Ali. I should've called Dennis to say I wasn't coming to the store for the sale. I should've done homework or watched the boys so my mom didn't have to deal with them at the grocery store or while she was cooking the holiday dinner they barely ate. But I didn't. I ate Junior Mints and let Brooks brand me with hickeys all over my body.

Monday afternoon I was crossing the street after school when Ricardo caught up with me.

"Gannon," he said, and grabbed my arm.

I shook him off. "What do you want?"

"Why'd you bail on the sale?"

"Um, because I quit."

He ran his hand over his stubby buzz cut and swore under his breath. "Okay, I'm not sure what happened between you and Dennis, but he's stomping around the store like a pissed-off rhino and when I even mentioned your name, he told me to get out. What the hell?"

I put my hands on my hips. "Did he also tell you he was a total asshole?"

His brow furrowed. "No, he didn't really mention that. It was more like, 'Gannon's on the highway to hell and you should stay as far away from her as possible.'"

"Nice. Very professional."

"So what happened?" He tucked his hands into his front

jeans pockets and waited. The short sleeves of his T-shirt stretched across his biceps. Ricardo was built, stocky in a wrestler kind of way. So different from Brooks's lankiness.

People walked by, nodding their heads and acknowledging Ricardo. No one said anything to me. Still Ricardo stared at me. Always so patient.

I released a sigh. "He told me I should stay away from Brooks."

"Classic." Ricardo laughed too hard. I gave him my death glare. "He's right though. You should. That guy's messed up."

"No, he's not."

Ricardo reached out and pushed aside the scarf around my neck. "Do your parents even notice these?" He didn't touch me, but I knew he was talking about the hickeys. "They look really bad."

"Go to hell." I moved toward the parking lot where the buses waited. Brooks had some outpatient rehab thing so he couldn't take me home and I was too ashamed to call Ali for a ride, even if she was back in school. Buses were the worst transportation known to man, but my boots had been giving me blisters all day and walking home would have destroyed my feet.

"Hey," Ricardo said, and grabbed my arm again. I shook him off. "You can't quit over this. You've been working there forever."

"Yes, in fact, I can. I don't need this crap. Dennis has no right to comment about who I'm dating."

"Wah, wah. Who gives a shit? You love work. Or at least you love getting out of your house." He looked at me with his too-perceptive eyes. "Apologize to Dennis for missing the sale and get your ass back there."

I swallowed a lump in my throat. Ricardo knew more about me than I'd realized. "I just can't be there right now."

I started to walk faster, praying he wouldn't follow me and ask more questions.

"Gannon," he called out. I turned back to him. "Don't decide right now. Give it a few days. You can make peace with Dennis later. And I'm sure Brooks wouldn't want you to give up your job for him."

I bit my lip. He would if it meant running away with him.

"I'll think about it," I called back. "No promises, though."

He nodded and grinned at me. "I'll work on Dennis in the meantime. You know he just said all that because he likes you and doesn't want to see you hurt."

"Once again, not his business." I raised an eyebrow. "Or yours."

"Message received," he said, then waved and trotted off back in the direction of school.

Dad was sitting in my room when I got home. Graying hair, tired face, too many wrinkles. And still the hesitant look in his eyes like he had no idea what the hell had gotten him to where he was. I was so surprised to see him seated on my bed I actually squeaked. He patted the spot next to him.

"I wanted to talk to you."

Oh Christ, they were getting a divorce.

"About what?"

"Your boyfriend, Michael," he answered. My jaw dropped. It was worse than the divorce talk. It was a Dad talk about Brooks. Pink flared on my cheeks.

"What about him?"

"Well, er," he said, and shifted uncomfortably on the bed. "I know you're almost eighteen and this is sort of your first boyfriend, so I want to make sure you're making the right choices."

I shut my eyes. *Please let me die right now.* "Is this a sex talk?" I whispered.

He nodded and shifted again. Had Mom put him up to this in anticipation of their weekend away?

"We trust you to make good decisions, but this boy seems to have become very important to you awfully fast, and I just wanted to let you know that if you have any questions, I'm here for you."

My eyes moved around the room. This was possibly the most horrifying moment of my life, in part because Dad had no idea how to have a sex talk and in part because he had no idea who I even was anymore. He wasn't *there* for me. He hadn't been *there* for any of us in a long time.

"Thanks, Dad. I'll keep you posted if I have any questions."

I hoped that would end the conversation and I could push him out of my room, but he'd gotten the whole thing in his head and apparently wanted to do it right.

"I got you some . . . protection if you need it."

"You bought me condoms? I don't . . ."

He stood and zipped out of my room. Seconds later he returned with a box of Trojans in his hand. "Take them. Let me know if you need more. There'll be no questions asked. I'd rather you be safe than sorry."

Holy hell, it was a nightmare of awkward parental conversations. It was the worst kind of ABC Family teen drama. I bit my lip and nodded at him.

"Okay. Thanks, Dad. I'm going to take a shower."

He leaped from my bed and hightailed it out of my room. Nothing mortified him more than the possibility of seeing his teenage daughter without clothes. It was why I knew I was always safe to cut.

I called Brooks as soon as Dad left the room. I needed his voice after the drama of the day. Ricardo. Dennis. My dad. I wanted to pour myself into him until it all went away. Until nothing was left but him, me, us.

"Hey. How'd it go with your appointment?" I asked when his gravelly voice picked up.

"Just fine. All clean and sober. That's a week since I've

been home from rehab and not one drug in my system. Sue's delighted."

"It *is* pretty impressive." I laughed as I heard him inhale what was probably his third cigarette in ten minutes. "How long do you have to keep taking drug tests?"

"Once a week while I'm still living with Sue."

"So much for our E plan."

He chuckled. "It was your E plan, sweetheart. If you recall, I was against you going there again. Not that you weren't awesome on E. But—"

"Yeah, yeah, compulsive personality. So you said."

"What did you do this afternoon?" he asked. I bit my lip, playing over my conversation with Ricardo. Was it fair to put all of that on Brooks? It wasn't my way, asking advice. Hadn't been my way for a long time. Neediness repulsed me.

"Dad gave me a sex talk and a box of condoms. Then told me to come talk to him if I needed some more."

Brooks choked on laughter and started to cough. "Fuck, yeah. Was it one of those value packs?"

"Shut up."

"Well, if it wasn't, you'll probably be pounding on his door for more in less than a week."

"You wish. And anyways, I'd rather bathe in a cauldron of hot, melted cheese then ask him to restock our condom supply. We can take care of our own protection, thank you."

"Sucker. Free is free. I'm busting into that box as soon as I come over on Friday night."

"I'm giving these back. We're buying our own condoms."

He laughed again. "Spoilsport." His voice dropped. "I wish it were Friday."

My heart thumped. The events of the day faded into the background. "My brothers will be here."

"Not worried."

I bit my lip again. Maybe it wasn't the best idea to have Brooks help me babysit. He could be incredibly distracting.

"You're too quiet," Brooks said. "You better not be backing out on me."

"Well . . . ," I started.

"I'm coming. Get used to it. Plus, you need my help."

I snorted. Brooks actually being helpful was about as likely as an ice cube freezing a lake, but I kept my doubts to myself.

"I've gotta go. I'll talk to you tomorrow."

"Okay," he said. "But real quick, what're you wearing?"

"Fuck off." I laughed and hung up.

16

My parents saw my brothers off at the bus on Friday morning and then gave me a long list of crap to do and a bunch of numbers I'd never use, except maybe 911, which I couldn't believe they'd actually written on the list. Then Mom gave me a tight hug and forced herself to get in the car. Dad smiled and winked at me.

I hoped for the sake of my brothers that their weekend alone helped things. I had my doubts, but if being together without the stress of my brothers improved their marriage, I was for it. Not that them being married or divorced made much of a difference in my life, but it would hurt my brothers if they split up. Their abandonment stuff ran deep, and even a dad phoning it in was better than no dad at all.

"So what're you doing this weekend?" Ali asked as I sat at our lunch table picking my sandwich apart.

We'd reached a tentative "don't ask, don't tell" agreement over the money situation. When I'd found her in the hallway to finally apologize for bailing on her, she'd refused to engage in a discussion about it and cut off all my questions with a clipped "I figured something out."

We were at the end of a table of Punkin' Donuts poseurs and Ali was painting her chipped nails black and ignoring the food next to her. Lunch always went this way. Ali had weird food allergies and barely ate enough to sustain a fly. I picked at the crappy pseudo–deli sandwiches the cafeteria made and then mostly ate cheese fries.

"My parents went out of town so I'm watching the boys."

"What? And you didn't tell me?"

"I thought you were grounded."

Ali flinched, but then slipped her "everything's fine" mask back on. "No. I told you I figured it out."

"Not with Skeevy Dave, though, right?"

She stared at her nails. "It's not your problem, Gannon. I took care of it. Now, are you having a party?"

My stomach tightened, but I didn't press any more. Ali wouldn't take the money from me now, even if I offered it. I rolled a piece of cheese into a ball and flicked it at her. "Did you miss the part where I'm watching my brothers? How can I have a party?"

She groaned. "Your parents are out of town and you're not having a party because of your brothers? You've got to be kidding me. Do you think they're gonna tell on you?"

"Not exactly. But I wouldn't put it past the little shits to drink half the supply in my parents' liquor cabinet and leave me to take them to the ER with alcohol poisoning."

Ali laughed. "Yeah. They probably would do that." She eyed me from beneath her too-long bangs. "Still. Seems like a waste not to take advantage of absent parents."

I rolled up another piece of sandwich. "Well, Brooks is coming over."

"Oh my God. You slept with him, didn't you? You promised to tell me," she said, too loud. Half the table turned their heads to look at us.

I flipped them off and hissed at Ali. "Jesus. Keep your voice down. You think I want all these losers up in my business?"

"They used to be your friends," she said, and there was a hint of accusation in her voice. Was she talking about herself too?

"No. They were never my friends. They don't know anything about me," I said, dropping my voice. "What's your problem? Is this about the money?"

She twisted the top back on to the nail polish. "No. And this is the last time I'm saying it: *I. Figured. It. Out.*"

"So why are you so prickly?"

"Listen, I don't give a shit who you hang out with. I'm just surprised, is all."

"Surprised about what?"

She blew her bangs out of her face and leaned forward. "Brooks bailed on you and then he shows up and all is forgiven. You were kind of a moody bitch when he was gone and I at least expected you to make him pay for taking off. But it's all just sunshine and roses with you two."

I snorted. "Sunshine and roses?"

She grinned. "Well, maybe tattoos and nipple rings, but you know what I mean."

"He was in rehab. It wasn't his fault he took off."

She drummed her fingers against the table. "Huh. Rehab for what?"

"His foster mom found his E."

She sighed. "Gannon. I'm not trying to be all judgmental. Really. But I didn't expect you to be that girl, you know? I mean, I get that there are things we don't tell each other or whatever, but still, you've kind of flaked on me for a guy, and that seems really un-Gannon."

I nodded. She was right. We weren't the sleep-over-and-do-mud-masks kind of friends, but still, I owed her more than just twenty minutes of bullshit chat at the lunch table.

"I might be in love with him," I said.

She shook her head. "Of course you are. The two of you are like frickin' Romeo and Juliet. Everyone knows it. We're just waiting to see which one of you takes the poison and which one takes a gun to his head."

"Nice."

She shrugged. "Just saying. This one isn't exactly a love story for the masses, you know?"

My hand moved to my stomach. The cut Brooks had made around my belly button had scabbed over, but I could still feel it. The one on the back of my thigh was messier, possibly even infected, but I didn't want to think about it.

"Yep. I know."

She looked at me for a long time before finally turning and dropping her nail polish into her bag. "Call me tomorrow morning. We can take your brothers to the House of Pancakes and then maybe to the rifle range so they can burn off a little excess energy."

I laughed and reached out for her hand. She drew it back and waved her fingers to indicate they were still wet. It was quick-dry polish, they weren't wet, but I had no right to say so. The gulf between us was still uncrossable.

I should have let it go, but I couldn't help saying, "So you don't have other plans in the morning?" *With Skeevy Dave.*

She heard the end of the sentence even if I didn't say it out loud. Her mouth pinched into a frown, but again she shook it off; then she lifted a shoulder and said, "I can work around things."

I nodded. "Okay. Sounds good."

• • •

My brothers were pathetically quiet when I picked them up from school. Mom had left me her minivan and asked that I drive the boys home instead of letting them take the bus so the day could seem more special. Staring at their sullen faces in the backseat almost made me burst out in laughter. This whole thing was about as special as root canal.

"So Mom left money for pizza," I said.

Luis snorted. "Can't trust you to turn an oven on but thinks you're fine to handle the three of us? Nice. Good to see how valuable we are."

"Shut up and stop acting like such a baby. It's one frickin' night. What're you so pissed about? That you don't get to terrorize Mom for twenty-four hours? Sorry to disappoint you."

Alex's mouth dropped open, but Luis didn't even blink. "Don't worry. We're not that pissed," he said, lifting his chin. "We'll just terrorize you instead."

I groaned. "And I'll tie you to your bedposts and lock you in your rooms without dinner." I grinned at them in the rearview mirror.

Miguel elbowed Luis and I bit my lip, trying not to laugh at the look of worry they shared. Maybe the night wouldn't be so bad after all.

Two hours later I was eating my words along with a pile of cheese on my plate. I'd let the boys serve up their own pizza and they'd pulled all the cheese off and divided up the dough between them, so I was left with a hill of mozzarella and my brothers' laughter.

I wanted to spit on their crust, but Mom's voice reminding me to make sure they ate pricked at my conscience. Their shouting and laughter calmed me so much more than their sullen silence in the car. Loud, annoying boys I could handle; the quiet ones were the problem. I stabbed the mass of cheese with my fork and then decided to dump the whole thing down the sink.

The doorbell rang and my heart thumped at the hope it was Brooks. Even if he wouldn't be any help to me, he was another body and could probably wrangle at least one of my brothers. The boys raced to the front door and whipped it open so it banged against the wall in the hallway.

Probably shouldn't have let them have Coke with dinner.

Brooks leaned against the doorjamb, wearing a too-big coat and holding three cans of Silly String.

"Boys," he said with a smile. He tossed a can at each of them. "Try not to waste it. I have a dozen more cans in the car, but they need to last the rest of the night."

My brothers squawked and snatched them from his hands, shaking the cans so the clicky noise filled the house.

"And for my girl," he said, and pulled out a DVD tucked in the inner pocket of his coat.

"*Halloween*. Classic. Good choice."

A stream of Silly String hissed in the background, followed by my brothers' familiar battle cry.

"They're gonna trash the place," I said, stepping toward Brooks.

He twisted his finger around a stripe of my hair and tugged me closer to him. "So?"

"I'm going to have to spend most of tomorrow cleaning."

I shivered as his tongue traced a line down my neck. "I'll help you," he whispered.

He pressed against me and I felt his hardness on my thigh. "Are you just gonna take me here with the door wide open so all the neighbors can see?"

He chuckled. "That was the plan."

"No." I pushed him away and clicked the door shut behind us. "Not with my brothers racing around."

He grabbed the neck of my shirt and pulled me into a tight hug. His freshly shaved face rubbed over the top of my head. "Okay. Okay. You win. I'll wait until they crash. Did you give them sugar?"

I grinned. "Yeah. And caffeine."

He moved toward the living room couch and plopped down, extending his feet onto our coffee table. "So it's gonna be a long night." He sighed.

Miguel raced past me and squirted a long pink string into Brooks's face. I laughed. "Yeah. Looks like it."

By ten o'clock the boys had fallen asleep in front of the TV. There was a twenty-four-hour *SpongeBob* marathon on and they'd vowed to stay up for it, but they'd lasted through only three episodes.

I shoved the pizza box into the trash and looked at the Silly String decorating the house. The boys had gone through all fifteen cans before they got distracted by *SpongeBob*. As I looked at their sprawled-out bodies draped over the couch, I eyed Mom's to-do list. How was I going to amuse them for an entire day?

Brooks slid behind me and pushed my hair away to expose the back of my neck. He nipped at it. "Finally asleep."

I nodded. He moved to his coat and pulled something out of his pocket.

"I have a surprise for you," he said with a grin.

"More Silly String?"

"Not quite."

I raised an eyebrow.

"Close your eyes," he said. I shut them and held out my hand. Moments passed. I heard a clicking noise. Then again and again.

"Ready?"

"Yep."

"Okay. Open your eyes."

The kitchen was alight with tiny candles. I beamed at Brooks. "Very sexy."

He licked his lips and moved toward me. "I thought you might like that. So are you in?"

"In for what?"

"Are you running away with me?"

My eyes darted to the couch to make sure my brothers were still asleep. "I haven't decided yet." I'd avoided the topic over the past week and Brooks hadn't pushed. Until now.

"It's a few months until my birthday. Even sooner till yours."

"You really think your dad would come after you, after all this time?"

"I don't know. Maybe. I'm always expecting him, but when I'm eighteen, I won't have anyone looking after me. No caseworker checking in. No Sue. I think he's waiting for that."

I nodded. It seemed unlikely, but who was I to say? Nothing about Brooks's life was anything I was familiar with.

"It could be both our birthday presents," he said, inching closer. The desperate look on his face made me want to bury myself in him. I could give him this. I'd planned to surprise him with a tattoo, but this could be so much better. Or so much worse.

"We're gonna need to make some plans," he continued. "Gather together our stuff. Kenji gave me a bunch of money, but you'll need to empty your bank account."

Money. Ali. Guilt warred inside me against a deep longing

to escape with Brooks. The dual emotions were terrifying, paralyzing.

"I thought you'd have decided by now," Brooks said. His voice hitched, and I couldn't tell if it was out of anger or hurt.

"It's a lot to consider. School, my brothers, my parents—"

"The parents who don't give a shit about you? Jesus, Gannon. Don't you love me?"

The words sat between us. I turned to look at the tiny candles. I did love him, but I'd never actually said it. It wasn't a word I used. It seemed too cliché for what we were about. And a tiny part of me didn't want to say it for fear of what it meant.

"Gannon?" He pressed his hands into my cheeks.

My tongue stuck to the roof of my mouth.

"Gannon?"

Our closeness was too much. I tried to turn away, but his hands stayed locked on my face. I pushed him back and his face changed to seething anger.

"Why won't you say it?" he snapped.

"Say what?"

He snarled and gripped me. "Tell me you fucking love me. Tell me all this drama has been worth something. God, at least give me that."

I bit down on my lip. Tears leaked from the corners of my eyes. What was my problem?

"Goddamn it. It was all for shit."

He stepped back and slammed his foot into the cabinet. My head whipped to my brothers to see if the noise had woken them, but they slept on, curled together like a litter of puppies. Brooks grabbed my wrist and pulled me away from the counter. He dragged me upstairs toward my parents' room and flung open the closet. I sat on the bed and pressed my knees into my face as he cursed and grabbed at the clothes hanging inside. I squeezed my eyes shut.

Pain and frustration clawed at me, attacking me from the inside out. Hundreds of needles of emotion pricked at my skin. I swallowed gulps of air and tried not to cry out. It was all too much.

Finally I heard a thump and then Brooks's loud exhale. I peeked at him. He stood in front of me with one of Dad's belts.

"Take it." He shook it in my face.

The pressure ratcheted up. I shook my head. He stepped closer and waved the belt in my face.

"Take it."

I reached out and skimmed my fingers over it but pulled them back. Brooks grabbed my wrist and shoved the leather into my hand. He dropped to the floor in front of me and pulled off his shirt so I could see his back.

"Hit me. Hold the opposite end of the buckle and hit me."

Tears streamed down my face. "What are you doing?" He was so exposed I didn't know what to do.

The part of me that still clung to the belief that parents take care of their children and that there was hope for a better life dwindled into nothing as I gazed at the planes of his back.

"What are you doing?" I asked again.

"Giving you everything." His words choked out of his mouth. "Now hit me."

My hand shook and I dropped the belt. How could he let me have this? And how could he think I'd ever want it? Everything overwhelmed me. The sob I'd been holding back broke out of me, more a moan now.

I wrapped myself around him. "I love you," I whispered. "I love you. I love you. I love you."

His body trembled. "Run away with me," he pleaded.

There was nothing anymore but this. Us.

I nodded and kissed him. "O-okay."

He pulled back and tugged on the hoops in my ear. Then his fingers moved down, following the lines of my face, brushing tears away. "It's going to be okay. I promise. Trust me."

My stomach wound into an even tighter knotted mess. "It's too fast."

"It's not."

"My parents won't forgive me," I whispered.

He rubbed his knuckles along my jaw. "They will." His fingers moved over the buttons of my shirt, undoing each one. My breath caught. He tugged my shirt off my shoulders, leaving me shivering in just a camisole. His teeth bit my shoulder at the strap. I sucked in a breath.

He started to peel off my cami, but I shook my head. "Not here. My parents fight here."

He nodded and lifted me into his arms, carrying me to my room. I clung to him, glancing at the recent school pictures of my brothers in the hallway. Mine was there too, taken so long ago I couldn't even remember what grade I'd been in. Third? Fourth, maybe?

Brooks dropped me onto my bed and pulled off my cami. He stood in front of me and stared. I blinked back at him, my eyes moving over the tattoo on his chest. It was peeling and looked even more painful than it had the first day. He rubbed his hand over it and then moved his fingers to the scars on my stomach.

There was too much to say. But I couldn't utter a word.

"I love you so much," he said.

I reached beneath my bed and pulled out a small package wrapped in Mom's silver holiday paper with a red bow on it. Brooks grinned at me as his fingers tore at the package.

"Early Christmas present?"

"Not exactly," I whispered.

He held my razor case in his open hand before shaking his head.

"No carving tonight," he said, and dropped the case onto the floor.

"It's not to cut."

"Are you giving this to me?"

I nodded. He stared at me, his eyes boring holes into every carefully placed barrier I'd ever put up. He saw into me. More than anyone ever had. It terrified me and at the same time bound me to him even more. There would be no hope of walking away from this unscathed without each other. We both knew it.

He knelt next to the bed and took my hand in both of his. "Tonight changes everything. Here. Now. I want to know exactly what you feel. I don't want you to hide behind pain. I want you to give it to me."

I rolled to my side and sat up. "I don't know what you're asking."

He grabbed my chin and turned me toward him. "Yes. You do. I want all of you. Everything. I don't want your feelings slipping out of you in drops of blood. I want them in me. I want to be part of it."

I scoffed, desperate to bring levity to the situation. "You're being melodramatic."

"Gannon," he said, and pulled me into his lap. "You know what I'm saying."

My breath had already started to grow shallow. My skin buzzed with anxiety and anticipation. "I don't think I can."

He gripped my hips too hard. "You can. You love me. You're running away with me. It's time to let me in. Please."

I started to shake. My fists tightened. I wanted to hit something. It felt too raw. My jeans rubbed against my infected thigh. I wanted to peel out of everything, even my own skin.

And then I was kissing him, grabbing him, clawing him. I bit his lip so hard I tasted blood. And still it wasn't enough. He held my hands and I scratched him. We rolled off the bed onto the floor, and it was a mess of too many emotions held inside for too long spilling out until I shook and sobbed and he curled himself around me.

"That's my girl," he whispered, kissing the tears from my cheeks. "That's what I wanted. Now it's mine too."

Tears poured from me again and he held me tighter. Then, exhausted from it all, we fell into a deep sleep.

17

It was the fire trucks that woke me, not the smoke. The faint faraway sound of sirens pierced through my foggy haze and I woke up, coughing. Smoke hung in the air above me, and at first I thought Brooks had lit a cigarette. But he was snoring beside me. I coughed again and shook him. His eyes blinked open.

"There's smoke," I said, still groggy. "Did you light a cigarette?"

He scrubbed the sleep from his eyes. Three passes of his hands over his face. Then he bolted up. "Gannon. That's not cigarette smoke." He moved to the door and grabbed the handle. He swore and drew his hand back. "It's a fire. We need to go out the window."

I stood then, comprehension jolting me. "My brothers!" I

shouted and moved toward the door. Brooks pulled me back.

"The fire's out there. The handle is burning up. We have to go out the window."

"No. My brothers are out there." I tore out of his grip and pulled the door open, ignoring the searing pain of the handle on my hand.

Flames leaped into the room, pushing me back. Brooks tackled me to the floor. His body covered mine. "We have to get out of here," he yelled over the roar of the fire.

He crawled to the window and pulled it open. The flames had grabbed on to my carpet and the room was filled with acrid smoke. Brooks tugged me toward him and tried to push me to the window.

"My brothers!"

"We'll get them," he yelled. "But we have to get out of here first."

He hoisted me toward the window and then I was falling. I tried to cling to the roof, but my hands slipped. I dropped to the ground and yelped. My ankle twisted beneath me. Pain and panic coursed through me. Brooks dropped next to me and pulled me into his lap.

"I hurt my ankle," I told him. "My brothers! Go get them."

Brooks looked at my awkwardly positioned foot and swore. Horns and sirens blared from the end of my block. Then firefighters were on us, everywhere.

One raced up to me and I screamed at him, "My brothers are inside. They were sleeping in the living room."

He nodded and motioned to two others heading into the flames. My whole house was lit up. Fire lapped at every window. The outside was charred, and the horrible smell of suffocating smoke was everywhere.

Brooks slipped his arm around my waist, lifting me gingerly. "We have to get out of here."

"What?" I turned on him. "My brothers are in there."

He raked his fingers through his hair. "I know. And they're going in to get them. But we've got to get out of here. This is our fault. They're gonna come after us."

"What do you mean? We didn't do anything." I was shrieking, my eyes trained on the front door, waiting for my brothers to emerge. It was taking too long.

"The candles," he shouted back at me.

My body went numb. Oh God. Had we done this? OhGodOhGodOhGodOhGod. My knees dropped to the ground. Brooks hauled me up.

"Gannon. We have to go," he yelled again.

I shook my head. "I can't leave them." Tears streamed down my face. "I have to get my brothers."

Brooks cupped my cheeks in his hands and stared into my eyes. "This isn't going to end well. We have to bolt."

"And do what? Leave them? What about my parents?" I asked, hiccupping through snot and tears.

"I don't know. We'll figure it out. But we have to go."

I shook my head. "They're my brothers."

Brooks smoothed his hand over my hair. "I know, baby. But I can't be wrapped up in this. I have a record. They'll send me back to juvie."

"It was an accident," I cried. "We didn't set fire to anything on purpose."

Brooks brushed at my tears. "That isn't how they'll see it. I wasn't even supposed to be here."

I opened and closed my mouth. Shouts came from behind me. Two firefighters burst out of the house, holding Miguel and Alex. Where was Luis? I shot up, ripping out of Brooks's hold, stumbling on my lame ankle.

I moved to the front door.

"Gannon," Brooks screamed after me. *"Gannon!"*

I barely registered the crowd of neighbors that had circled the sidewalk along the side of my house. I could only think about Luis. Still inside. I held my hand over my nose and blinked through the smoke pouring out of the front door. Voices screamed from different places. Firefighters on the right side of my house, hosing out flames. More by the truck, barking orders to one another. I pushed my way in, then dropped to my knees and started crawling toward the living room couch. I realized he wasn't there as soon as I saw the entire thing was covered in flames.

"Luis!" I shouted.

Nothing.

"Luis!" I yelled again, coughing.

A tiny voice cried out from the corner of the room. I made my way toward it and found Luis with a blanket wrapped around him. His black eyes blinked in terror. I reached out to him and threw the blanket over his head, telling him not to breathe too deeply. I was coughing so hard I wasn't sure he even understood me.

I gripped his thin body, pulling him in to me, and started to move toward the door. My ankle dragged behind me. I almost couldn't feel it anymore. My head hurt and I was sweating. My eyes were watering so much I couldn't make out anything in the room. I buried my face in Luis's blanket and crawled forward, feeling his fingers cling to my shoulders through the scratchy fabric. The distance to the front door seemed like miles now. I had to stop to cough, trying desperately to rid my lungs of the burning. I got dizzy and leaned back. Luis dug his fingers in deeper. My brain screamed at me to move, but my lungs wouldn't release me from the endless coughing.

Then the fog overtook me and I fell forward. The floor felt

surprisingly cool against my cheek. I didn't feel Luis's fingers anymore, but I knew he must be nearby.

"Go," I tried to say to him, but it was too soft. Maybe I didn't even say it at all.

I blinked two more times and closed my eyes.

"*Gannon!*" I thought I heard, but knew it was just the smoke clouding over me. Even still, I smiled for a second before the blackness pushed at the corners of my eyes and there was the pleasantness of nothing.

I woke feeling like I was buried alive. My arms tried to flail, but they were strapped to my sides. I was enveloped in gauze, and every part of me itched so much I shifted back and forth to ease it.

"Amelia," Mom breathed from the space beside me. I turned my head and she gave me a tiny smile.

"You look like shit," I said to her. My voice sounded like my throat had been stripped of its vocal cords.

She laughed once and wiped her red splotchy face. "So do you."

My hands pressed against the straps. "Why am I tied up?"

"What happened?" Mom countered.

"How am I supposed to know?" The cloud of the evening pressed against my brain. I coughed too hard and Mom stared at me with frightened eyes. "Where's Brooks?" I finally asked when I could breathe again.

Mom pursed her lips and shifted in her chair. "Why was he at the house last night?"

"Last night? What time is it?"

"It's a little after three in the afternoon."

"Why am I tied up?" I asked again. My hands fisted. I stared out the hospital window into late-afternoon gray. The events of the night played like a movie in my head. Too fast. Too many images. Too many questions. I coughed again. "Did Luis get out?"

Mom nodded. "He's with Dad down the hall. You were smart to wrap him in the blanket. He inhaled much less smoke than you."

I coughed again and shifted my body to relieve the itching on my back. "Untie me."

"You have a bad sprain in your ankle. And the burns on parts of your legs are pretty bad. But they think they'll be able to fix them. It'll take a while. They'll have to do some skin grafting."

I looked down. I couldn't feel my legs. They were hidden by gauze and I couldn't feel them. Not good. "So you tied me up so I wouldn't freak over my legs?"

Mom chewed on her bottom lip. She leaned toward me and touched my face. "The doctors, they saw all the cuts and scars. They're concerned you're a danger to yourself." Her voice cracked and a sob erupted from her throat. "How long have you been doing that?"

I swallowed and looked away. It was going to rain. The clouds were fat and ready to burst. A tear slipped out of my left eye.

"Amelia," she whispered, "did you . . . did you set the fire on purpose? Were you trying to kill yourself?"

I shook my head back and forth too many times. More tears leaked out. Where was Brooks?

"How long have you been cutting yourself?" Mom asked again, firmer this time, determined to push forth something real between us.

I turned away from her and shut my eyes. It was too late for her questions. Too late to ask for anything more than the kindness of lying. The hospital window speckled with the first drops of rain, and I stared out, aching for Brooks and offering Mom nothing but loaded silence.

Finally she stood up and moved toward me, eyes darting to the dressings on my legs. I couldn't look at them. Didn't care about them. More scars. More damage. None of it mattered.

"We need to have a conversation at some point," Mom said. Her fingers skimmed over the hair plastered to my forehead. I flinched and pressed back into the pillow, straining against the straps on my wrist again.

"Release my wrists."

She tucked a piece of my hair behind my ear. "Why did you cut yourself?"

I blinked back angry tears and turned my face to the window again. I shut my eyes, praying for sleep that wouldn't come, praying for Brooks to walk in and save me from the reality of this life.

18

I was in the burn unit of the hospital for ten days before they moved me. Ten days of no one telling me where Brooks was. Ten days of having my every move monitored. Ten days of itching and screaming and then finally silence. My parents wouldn't let anyone visit me. They said they were worried about infection. Then one morning a nurse came in and helped me out of bed and wheeled me to the psych unit. Like it was nothing. Like they transferred mental patients all the time.

Then began the incessant talking. Hours of talking. Individual and group therapy every day. Inpatient psych was more of a joke than any crappy TV drama I'd ever seen. At first I kept my mouth shut and stared out the window, but then one of the therapists told me I'd just have to stay longer. So I talked about my family, my brothers, school, Brooks. And I waited for someone to tell me what had happened. But they wouldn't.

Mom and Dad and the boys came to family therapy and I listened as the boys accused me of not looking out for them. Mom said she was angry I hadn't told her about the cutting. Dad yelled at Mom for not paying enough attention to me. I told them all they could rot in hell.

Finally, a few days after Christmas, Ali got to come see me. She'd streaked her hair pink and was wearing a half shirt showing off her belly button ring. She hugged me so hard when she saw me I coughed. She dropped her arms and looked at me in fear.

"I'm fine. You just squeezed too tight."

She relaxed and plopped onto the plastic visitor couch. "I've missed you, bitch."

I grinned at her and wrapped my pinkie around hers. "Me too. How come it took you so long to come?"

She opened her mouth. "Are you shitting me? I've had to plant myself at your parents' door and beg them every frickin' day to let me come see you."

I blinked. Of course. My parents. I should have known they wouldn't let anyone in to see me. My heart squeezed. Brooks. Was he trying to get to me too?

"Where's Brooks?"

She looked at her hands and dropped her voice. "I'm not supposed to tell you. It was the only way to get your parents to agree to me visiting."

I shifted toward her. "Screw that," I said. "Tell me now."

She clicked her tongue piercing. "Okay. But don't freak out. If you freak out, they'll know I told you and I'll never get back in here."

I folded my hands in my lap. "I'm listening."

"He's back in juvie."

"What?" I stood up and knocked the table in front of me. The nurse at the front desk looked up at us.

Ali waved at her and yanked me back down. "Shh, calm down. You aren't supposed to freak out."

"What's he doing in juvie?"

Ali leaned toward me. "How much do you remember about what happened the night of the fire?"

"Most of it. At least up until I blacked out trying to get Luis out."

She nodded. "Brooks tried to go in after you, but a firefighter held him back because the flames were out of control at that point. Finally he hit the guy and ended up breaking a window to get in and drag you out. The firefighter had him taken into custody. And then things got really bad. I guess your parents showed up and went nuts. Obviously. Brooks was brought in and charged for reckless child endangerment."

"What?" I shouted, and Ali slapped a hand across my mouth.

"Can you please calm down?"

I nodded my head and she released her hand. "Sorry."

"So yeah, I guess he had some kind of stipulation on his earlier probation. After he assaulted the firefighter and then they found out he'd been to rehab," Ali continued, and she raised an eyebrow at me, "they sent him back to juvie. It was actually sort of lucky they didn't try him as an adult. I guess his foster mom convinced the police not to."

"Oh my God," I said and twisted my hands together. "I have to do something. It wasn't his fault."

"He told them he lit the candles and forgot to blow them out. He admitted everything."

"Why would he do that?"

She lifted a shoulder. "I think he was trying to protect you."

"He didn't light the candles to burn the house down, though. It wasn't arson."

Ali nodded. "I know. That's why the prosecutors went with child endangerment. Your parents don't want him anywhere near you or the boys. They think he's a bad influence."

I snorted. "I had my razors long before I ever met Brooks."

The truth of my words sat between us. Ali toyed with the chain at her neck before finally nodding. "You need to get out of here, Gannon. Get yourself better. Do whatever they tell you."

"I'm trying, Ali."

She hooked her arm in mine. "Try harder. I can't have my best friend in the nuthouse. It looks bad."

I stared hard at her. "Am I still your best friend?"

"Of course."

"I'm sorry I didn't give you the money."

She clicked her tongue again and nodded. "Jace did."

"Really? I thought you were going to have to help Skeevy Dave out."

A side of her mouth tilted up. "Yeah. I kinda wanted you to think that. But Jace wouldn't hear of it. He gave me what he had saved up and then borrowed against his paychecks for the rest." She laughed, but it came out forced and awkward. "Lucky his boss likes him so much."

"Are you gonna owe him something now?"

She shrugged. "He told me I could pay him back this summer when I get a job."

I squeezed her elbow. "Okay. Just be careful. I don't want him pushing you into doing something because you feel like you have to pay off a debt."

She raised her eyebrows at me. "Dating advice from the girl whose boyfriend managed to burn her house down."

Brooks. Every cell in my body ached for him. The craving was worse than anything I'd ever felt before, worse even than when I was so desperate for my razors I couldn't think straight.

"When you get out," Ali continued, "you'll figure out how to help him. But don't say anything to your parents about any of this. They blame him for everything. You won't be able to change their minds."

She was right, of course. My parents would never trust anything I said about Brooks. Especially after they found out about the cutting. My anger at what they'd done burned inside of me. I had to get out and help Brooks, and I had to do it on my own. I hugged Ali.

"If you see him, hear from him, whatever, tell him I love him."

She rolled her eyes but then nodded. "Just get yourself out of here."

It was six more weeks before they released me. Six weeks, thirty-six individual therapy sessions, twenty-one group therapy sessions, and two more painful family sessions.

The last family session involved a full-on screaming match about Brooks. About my dating him. About what the charges against him meant. I almost blurted out that he'd probably be stuck with probation, unable to leave if his dad came after him, but decided against it. My parents didn't care. They only cared about me never seeing Brooks again. At the end of the session they dropped the bomb that they'd requested a restraining order against him seeing me. After that I stopped talking about him. I was a shell; nothing they said or did could convince me I was better off without Brooks. So I stared through them and dropped their meaningless words into a space inside me filled with years of their fake bullshit platitudes about the importance of "family."

Before I left the hospital, I had more than a dozen consultations about the burns on my legs. I didn't care about them. More scars. More battle wounds. My body was littered with lines and marks and none of them seemed nearly as painful as the emotional damage of losing Brooks.

I checked out of the psych unit wearing scrubs, a pile of resources tucked into a plastic bag on my lap as they wheeled me past the pale peach walls of the hospital. I had to keep seeing a therapist, keep taking antidepressants, and my family was given the task of finding a family therapist we liked enough to show up for appointments.

Dad had found us a furnished apartment. The walls were industrial tan and the furniture reeked of wet dog. My room was right next to my parents', of course. Mom had picked up three pairs of jeans and some T-shirts from the Gap and put them into the drawers of the crappy plastic dresser along with some underwear and tank tops. I wanted to barf when I thought of all the clothes I'd lost in the fire, but I slid into her replacements without saying a word. They were better than the hospital scrubs I'd been wearing for too long.

Things with my brothers were weird. They didn't know how to be with me. They'd worked out some kind of temporary truce with Mom and Dad, but they seemed to be walking on eggshells around me. Mostly I ignored everyone and sat on the roof of our new building, practicing how to roll Indian Spirit cigarettes. My parents checked on me often but didn't say anything about the smoking. Guess they decided cigarettes were better than razors.

I was supposed to go back to school, but I convinced my therapist to buy me until the end of the school year. My teachers agreed to let me continue with "virtual school" while I recovered. The hospital staff had forced me to keep up with my studies in the psych unit, so my grades had actually improved. It was about the only interesting thing to do there anyway.

I spent my first nights at home researching ways I could help Brooks, but nothing looked promising. I was seventeen, with not enough money to hire any legal help. I considered going to Dennis and asking to borrow money, but I hadn't seen him since the day I walked out, and even though my parents said he'd called to check on me a bunch of times, I couldn't reach out to him.

Ricardo stopped by, but I barely looked at him as he fidgeted on the crappy leather couch. He told me funny things about the store and did the uncomfortable talking thing until I told him to go. He offered to come back, but I told him I wasn't really up for company yet.

I watched classic horror movies over and over. I stared at the fake blood and bad actors and longed for Brooks.

· · ·

Ali came to visit on my birthday. She was the only one I could stomach seeing, because she'd told me the truth. She brought me some clothes from Dark Alley, which was only a minor improvement over the Gap, and a bright red card with no name on the front.

"Thanks," I said, slicing my finger when I opened the envelope. A drop of blood formed on the tip, and I stared at it. The rush I'd always gotten when I felt pain and saw my own blood had disappeared. When had that happened?

Ali watched me. "You're welcome. I thought this would make you happy."

I raised an eyebrow and slid the card from the envelope. My breath caught as soon as I opened it.

Gannon,

Twenty-six days, nineteen hours, forty-one minutes. Give or take. I'll be coming for you. You know what I want. You better be ready.

Brooks

My hands shook and a stupid grin formed on my face.

"How did you get this?"

"My mom dumped Skeevy Dave and started dating this juvenile probation officer named Mike. He's grown kind of fond of Brooks, apparently."

"You're shitting me." I stared at her. "Why didn't you tell me that in the first place? You could have been getting messages to him."

She held up her hands and shook her head. "It's a pretty new relationship for Mom, and Mike's not exactly a rule breaker. This was kind of a big deal and I had to beg for weeks to get him to mention to Brooks that I could pass a message to you."

"I can't believe it." I read the card again.

"You're welcome."

I jumped on her and hugged her. "You're the best friend ever."

"Whoa. Don't strain yourself. That's more exercise than you've had all month."

"Very funny." My fingers moved over the letters on the card again.

"His ass better be worth all this," she grumbled, but then winked at me.

Mom and Dad must have expected it, somewhere deep down. They knew Brooks would be released from juvie when he turned eighteen. And no amount of family therapy could change the fact that they'd lost part of me when they'd adopted the boys and the rest of me when they'd gotten a restraining order against my boyfriend. It was easy for me to let go of them completely.

And I couldn't deny that my brothers needed them more than I ever had.

Since I'd been home from the hospital, Miguel had started to steal money off my parents' dresser and Luis had been given a three-day suspension for fighting in school. Mom looked more worn down than ever, and Dad spent two to three nights a week "working" past midnight.

Every day Mom asked if I wanted to get more clothes, but I just shook my head and sat on the roof, wrapped in my thick winter coat, waiting. Ali visited a few times a week. She brought me clothes and told me stories about Jace and the poseurs at Dark Alley. She told me Probation Officer Mike said Brooks was doing okay. I begged Mom to let me visit him, but she refused. She claimed "the officials" wouldn't agree to it. Maybe she was right. I didn't think she bothered trying.

Mom had me on lockdown. Mandatory "family time" every night. No visits for me outside the house unless she drove and waited for me or I was going to therapy. I watched time pass in the grayness of the sky, the iciness of snowflakes, and the evenness of my breaths.

Cigarette smoke coiled around my head as I stared at the setting sun. The time for Brooks's release had passed two days ago and still no word. I asked Ali, but she didn't know anything. Probation Officer Mike was staying mute about it.

Now Dad was "at work" and Mom was "running around with the boys." I stood alone, relishing the hour a day to myself that I craved like an addict. The hour I'd begged for and "earned" through attending crap family therapy. Winter had always depressed me with its short days, but I'd come to love the cold silence and the grayness of five o'clock.

A sharp whistle below pierced the quiet and I stared into the dusk.

"That better be Indian Spirit."

I dropped my cigarette. "Brooks!" I shouted, and bolted to the fire escape on the side of the building. My feet couldn't move down the iron rungs fast enough. My lungs burned and my heart thumped, a staccato rhythm of *Brooks. Brooks. Brooks.*

My legs ached where the burns had turned to scars, but none of it mattered compared to the boy standing on the sidewalk beneath me. He had on jeans and a T-shirt, and his eyes followed my movement down the ladder.

"It's frickin' freezing outside. What the hell are you wearing?" I screamed at him.

"I thought you might offer to warm me up." He smiled and my insides turned to liquid heat.

My feet hit the ground and then I was in his arms, my legs locked around his waist, kissing his face everywhere. My teeth found his bottom lip and I tugged him closer to me, driving my tongue into his mouth. He groaned and laughed at the same time.

"That's my girl."

I pushed his faded blue hair back and traced his face with my fingers. Cool, smooth skin and too-obvious bones. My thumbs moved over the deep purple circles beneath his eyes. "I missed you."

"I know."

I stopped tracing and gripped his cheeks. "I know? I know? That's it?"

"Yeah." He released me and tucked my hair behind both ears. His fingers moved to the zipper of my coat and tugged. Then he pulled at the collar of my shirt and searched out the hollow beneath my collarbone.

"Not so fast." I put my hand on top of his. "Now would be the time for you to mention you missed me too."

"Hmm . . . ," he murmured, and dipped his tongue into the spot his fingers had been circling. He started to suck and I swatted at him.

"Brooks."

"Gannon."

"Say you missed me."

He lifted his head up and his breath tickled the hoops on my ears, making me shiver. My hands slipped inside his shirt and I walked my fingers up to the now smooth tattoo on his chest.

"You know I did," he whispered.

"Say you love me."

"I love you."

I grinned at him. "I love you too."

"Yes. Yes, you do."

I stared at him for a long time, memorizing his features, drinking him in. My fingers played over his chest.

"Are you ready?" he asked, and leaned down so his hot breath tickled my neck.

"You still want me to go with you? Even after everything I put you through? Even knowing what it means if they catch you?"

He nipped and sucked my neck until I could almost feel the hickey popping out. Then he pressed his hand onto mine so my palm flattened against the thumping of his chest. "I'm here, aren't I? Five o'clock. The hour of your daily release."

"Ali told you," I said with a grin.

He nodded and patted my hand. "Yes. And see, I've come for you. Because no one else could make you bleed like me."

I slid my hand out from beneath his shirt and wrapped my arms around his neck, pulling him closer to me. "You should see my new scars."

"I will. Every single one of them."

"Wait here," I said, and kissed the end of his nose.

I jogged up to my apartment and snatched the bag I'd had packed and tucked into the closet for the past few weeks. It wasn't very full, but it had the clothes Ali had brought me as well as all the money from my hardware savings account, cleared out one afternoon when I was walking home from therapy. As I stomped through the living room, I caught a glimpse of a framed picture of my family out of the corner of my eye. In a quick move I snatched it and tucked it into my bag before pounding back downstairs, grateful everyone was at work or at their afternoon activities.

Brooks sat on the hood of his car, shivering.

"The Civic still runs?" I asked.

He grinned at me. "Yeah, Ray drove it while I was in juvie."

A lump formed in my throat at the mention of his past few months. And I wondered again if he was okay.

He snatched my bag from me and tossed it in the back-seat next to his black duffel bag. He grabbed one of the belt loops on my jeans and guided me toward the passenger door before pulling it open and sliding me in. He bounced around to his side and started the car. It hiccupped, coughed, and then finally purred to life.

"And we're off," he said. He pointed to the glove compartment, and I popped it open to find a carton of filtered menthols. "Just in case you weren't able to kick the habit yet."

I leaned over and rifled through my bag until I found the bag of Indian Spirit cigarettes I'd rolled. "I've kicked the habit," I said, shaking the bag in his face and smiling too wide.

"Thank God." He reached over and squeezed my hand.

"So where to?" I asked.

He turned to me and stared. It was like he was memorizing every part of my face. I blushed from my striped hair to my toes.

"Don't know. Where do you want to go?"

I opened my mouth. He didn't have a plan? Panic gripped me for several seconds. I stared at the dashboard in front of me with all its cracks and dings. It wasn't his fault. He'd just gotten out. He got out and came for me. It was all that mattered. He squeezed my hand again and I looked up.

"So?" he asked.

The tiny lump in the back of my throat had turned into a soccer ball. I choked it down and took my turn to memorize his face. The face I'd missed so much, the face I'd dreamed about, now thinner and more guarded. "Just drive," I said, my voice too low. I cleared my throat and tried again. "We'll figure it out."

PART II

19

Apparently, if you want to hide from a potentially psychotic father with a penchant for taking swings at caseworkers or a messed-up family who watched your every move like you were a circus freak, you go to Minneapolis. Or at least that's where Brooks and I ended up. Seven hours in his crappy Civic, listening to Ray's white-boy-rap CDs and smoking all the Indian Spirit rolled cigarettes I'd packed. Minneapolis was far enough for me.

"It's a big city. Not Chicago big, but still easy to get lost in," I said, pointing to the handful of skyscrapers on the horizon of downtown Minneapolis.

"Less than a day's drive from Chicago, though."

"I gotta get out of this car. Even if this isn't home for us, we have to stop here."

Brooks nodded and pulled into the parking lot of a sad-looking Comfort Inn with a vacancy sign.

"You're gonna have to learn to sleep in the car some, sweetheart. It's not exactly in the budget to be doing hotels every night."

I bit my lower lip. "Maybe we could find a place to live here. Jobs and stuff." My phone buzzed in my pocket for the four hundredth time since we left.

"Goddamn it," Brooks snarled, snatching my phone. "Enough already." He pulled out the SIM card and plopped the phone back in my lap.

Mom had stopped trying to get through after the first hour of straight-to-voice-mail and had now taken to leaving pleading texts every ten minutes. I'd called Ali to let her know I'd taken off and asked her to let Mom know I was fine. Then in a shaky voice I'd told Ali I'd miss her and ignored the disapproval and worry in her response.

"I can sleep in the car. Just not tonight. Not the first time I have you back."

Brooks grinned at me, and my sulkiness over his lack of plan dissolved a bit. "Point taken. I'll be right back." He dropped a kiss on my cheek.

Fifteen minutes later we were wrapped up in each other, rolling on the crunchy polyester Comfort Inn bedspread, hands and mouths fighting for access.

"I missed you," I said, pulling away and breathing hard. "God, I missed you so much."

"Me too." He nipped at my collarbone.

"We should get something to eat," I whispered. My arms circled around him one last time before I rolled away. "You've got to be starving."

His head rose. "Not for food."

I swatted him. "Don't be gross. We haven't eaten all day. Why don't you pick something up?"

"This is on me? Don't you have cash?"

I sat up on my elbows. "Yeah, don't you?"

"Yeah. But it's your turn."

"What do you mean it's my turn? I bought the cigarettes."

"So did I. Your crappy menthol ones, no less. And I paid for gas when we stopped." He squinted at me and something twisted inside. This new guarded and slightly hostile part of Brooks scared me.

I bit my lip. "Sorry. I'm sorry. I don't want to fight with you. I'll buy dinner." I shimmied off the bed and held my hand out for the car keys.

He sat up. "Now? You're gonna go now? I thought you were tired of being in the car."

"I am, but I'm hungry and you just said it's my turn."

Brooks shook his head. "Seriously? You're gonna leave me here so you can get food? I haven't seen you in months."

I blinked at him. "But I ran away with you. I'm not going anywhere. I just want some food."

"Fine. Go get some food." He pulled his wallet out of his pocket and threw a twenty-dollar bill at me, then tossed the keys at my feet.

I shook my head and wished we hadn't smoked the last cigarette in the car. "I said I'd pay. Why are you getting all pissed off?"

He quirked an eyebrow. "Why do you think?"

"Don't make this into a big deal. I'm hungry. I'm starting to get a headache from lack of food."

His fingers brushed his hair from his eyes. "It *is* a big deal. I want to be with you and you only care about eating." Anger switched to sad eyes that bored into me. "Can't you just stay with me for a little while? Please."

I nodded and moved toward him, a strange pull drawing me back, making me ignore my hunger headache. My fingers traced his face, smoothing out the line on his forehead that hadn't been there a few months ago. He grabbed my fingers and stuck them in his mouth, sucking hard. I sat on his lap and wrapped myself around him, feathering his face with kisses, stopping myself from ruining everything by asking him what the hell had happened in juvie.

Coffee from Dunn Brothers tasted like ass in comparison to the Punkin' Donuts coffee. I dumped more cream and another pack of sugar into my cup and watched as Brooks leafed through the classifieds.

"Okay, if you really have your heart set on staying, we need to find some work," he said.

"Are you qualified to do anything?" He winced and I immediately regretted my words. "I'm kidding. How come you're so sensitive?"

"I'm not sensitive. I'm just trying to figure out a way for us to live in the manner you've grown accustomed to, princess."

"Go to hell. I'm so far from being a princess it's not even funny and you know it."

He grinned. "I don't know, Gannon. I heard you ask the lady at the front desk if the eighty-nine-dollar rate was for weeknights only. Sounds like you're planning an extended stay at the Comfort Inn."

I stared into my coffee cup. If the alternative was sleeping in the Civic, then yes, I was. "Do you see any job prospects?"

"There's a bunch of waitressing stuff. Do you have any experience with that?"

"No. You know I've only ever worked at the hardware store."

He drummed his fingers on the overly polished wooden table. "We haven't talked about what you've been doing lately. For all I know, you got a job working at TGI Fridays."

His words stung. They shouldn't have, but they just punctuated the fact that we weren't the same Brooks and Gannon. Why did this feel so hard? "Brooks. The only thing I've been doing lately is waiting for you."

Half his mouth turned up and he grabbed my hand from across the table and squeezed. "Really? So you haven't moved on with your life, peddling buffalo wings and mozzarella sticks while flirting with a bartender named Steve who plays in a wedding band on the weekend?"

I fake gagged. "Please. I'd rather donate an egg than be caught dead in a TGI Fridays."

He patted my hand. "That's my girl." He returned to the classifieds. "They're looking for counter help at a Pizza by the Slice. I think you should apply there. I've seen the staff at the one in Chicago and I don't think they're too particular about hair and piercings. They'll probably even pay you under the table."

My arms folded. "Why don't you apply there?"

He lowered the paper. "Because I'm not a girl. If I get a job, I guarantee I won't be working the front counter."

"If?"

He gulped down the rest of his coffee and raised a shoulder. "I called Kenji while you were in the bathroom this morning. He knows some guys here. I might be able to work for them."

My teeth bit down on the inside of my cheek. The coffee

sat like battery acid in the pit of my stomach. "Guys? Like deal-ers?" I whispered. Brooks nodded once. "Is that really the best idea after you've just gotten out of juvie?"

He folded the paper and put it to the side. "My girl needs a place to live. That's not going to pay for itself."

Guilt wound itself around me and squeezed. My skin itched and tingled for the first time in a long while, but I tamped down the craving for pain. This was our life now and I needed to be realistic about it. I dug my fingernails into my palm and nodded.

"Let's see if I can find a job first."

"You're not gonna be stuck covering rent on your own," he said. "I'll look for a job too. Something that pays under the table so they don't find out I'm in violation of my probation."

"It might be easier if I just—"

He held his hand up. "We're in this together. I'm not gonna be some kept man at home while my woman goes to work."

I stood up and winked at him, desperate to lighten things between us. "Maybe that's the way I want you. At home, ready and waiting."

A low grunt escaped Brooks's lips. "We should go back to the hotel. Now."

I smiled at the return of Brooks. My Brooks. I grabbed his hand and let his need for me block out everything else.

20

Brooks was right. As soon as the manager at the Pizza by the Slice figured out that I had basic math skills and spoke English, he hired me. He didn't even bat an eye when I asked to be paid in cash. I thought I might have to pull out Dennis as a reference and dreaded all that would come with that, but he didn't ask for anything other than me to be at work at eleven the next morning.

I was so thrilled I splurged on Chinese takeout and brought it back to the hotel room.

"Jesus, you know how to burn through money," Brooks said the minute I walked in the door with the bag.

"It's fried rice. It barely costs anything."

He pursed his lips. "At this rate we'll have to move back to Chicago and live with your parents before the month is out."

I'd convinced Brooks to stay at the Comfort Inn for three nights. The idea of sleeping in the Civic in the middle of March in Minnesota was about as appealing as plucking my fingernails out with tweezers. He guilted me about how we didn't have the money, but I wouldn't budge. I planned to find a less-expensive youth hostel to move into before the end of the week.

"I got the pizza job," I said, dropping the food next to the TV on the dresser. "Minimum wage, but it's forty hours a week and he'll pay me under the table."

Brooks pulled me down and kissed me. "That's my girl."

"Did you find anything?"

He looked away for a second and worry wound itself inside me. "No," he said, turning back, "it's not so easy for guys. Especially finding work where you don't need any references and want to be paid cash."

I wanted to cry bullshit on that, but maybe he was right; maybe girls did have it easier. "We should figure out how much rent we can afford based on my minimum wage and our savings." When had I become so practical?

He curled a piece of my hair around his finger. "I found a place for us."

"What?" I pushed up. "Already? Without me even having the job yet? How?"

"I met these two guys. They're professional waiters. They said we could stay with them."

I closed my eyes and sighed. "Brooks. You met some guys? We don't know anything about them. We can't just move in with a couple of randoms and think everything is going to be fine. They could be serial killers."

"Jesus, Gannon. What the hell happened to you when you were in the hospital? Where's the girl who asked me to slice open the back of her thigh?"

My body curled into itself. Where was the boy who was afraid he hurt me when he did?

"We're gonna have to take some risks if we're gonna make this work," he continued. "These guys aren't serial killers. They're nice guys. Gary and Bruce. Their roommate moved out and they said we could take the spare bedroom. Rent's two-fifty a month. That's dirt cheap. What did you expect me to do? A background check? It's not like they're doing one on us."

I rolled off the bed and moved to the bathroom.

"Gannon," he called after me. "Don't fucking walk away from me."

I stared at myself in the mirror. The giddiness from getting a job had drained out of me and now I looked worn down. Too pale, too thin, too overwhelmed. For a second Mom's face flashed in the mirror, and I stepped back, guilt sloshing around like an overly full cup inside of me.

"Gannon," Brooks snarled from the doorway. "Talk to me."

"I'd like to meet them first," I said, voice shaky.

He stepped forward and wrapped his arms around me. "Of course you will, sweetheart. They said we could go over later tonight and check the place out."

I nodded. He tucked me beneath his chin and smoothed my hair. "Tell me this will all be okay," I whispered.

He lifted my chin. "It'll be okay. We're together. It's all we need."

The minute I met Gary and Bruce, my two future roommates, six hundred warning bells went off in my head. One answered the door to the tiny basement apartment in cutoff jean shorts and a flannel shirt. His full head of hair was combed back into some sort of pompadour thing. He held a leg of barbecue chicken in one hand. Some of the barbecue sauce was still on his chin.

"Brooks," he yelled, holding his hand out for a high five. Brooks raised his eyebrows but then gave him the high five and walked in. "And this must be Gannon."

I nodded. "Nice to meet you."

"I'm Gary and this is Bruce." He pointed to a guy sitting on a couch, watching TV with a large mop bucket of barbecue chicken next to him.

Bruce wiped his fingers on the bib circling his neck and smiled at us. His double chins shook as he spoke. "We're so stoked you guys are coming to live with us. It's been forever since we had a chick around here."

Gary snorted. "Speak for yourself, my man."

"Dude, I'm not talking about your sister," Bruce answered, and waggled his eyebrows at me. *Oh God. Kill me now.*

Gary dropped the half-eaten chicken leg into the mop bucket and rubbed his hand on the couch. I stole a glance at Brooks, who shrugged.

"So you wanna see the place?" Gary gestured to the couch, TV, and army trunk serving as a coffee table. "This is the living room, where we entertain." He winked at me and pointed to the two closed doors on the side of the living room. "And those are the bedrooms."

"No kitchen?" I asked.

Bruce chimed in from behind me. "Nah. But we work at a restaurant, so we don't really need one." He pointed to the yellow bucket beside him. "We also barbecue a lot."

"Where's the bathroom, then?" I asked, eyeing the closed doors. Evidently, we were all going to have to share one. I hoped I wouldn't have to traipse through Gary and Bruce's room to pee in the morning.

"No bathroom, either," Bruce said.

My eyes widened and I glared at Brooks. Gary looked between the two of us.

"You didn't tell her, huh?" Gary asked Brooks.

Brooks tucked his hand in his jeans pocket. "The place isn't totally up to code, but Bruce and Gary are willing to let us stay here and will take cash for rent. There's a bathroom at the McDonald's across the street."

I swallowed. A bathroom at the McDonald's? This was my life?

Gary winked at me again, and for a second I wondered if he had some sort of eye condition. "Listen, we know you all are sort of 'on the lam,'" he said. Sweet Jesus, he was doing air quotes. "And we won't ask any questions if you don't. It'll all be good. You have a place to stay. We get a little help with the rent. Win-win."

I spun on my heel and snatched Brooks's elbow. "Can I talk to you for a second outside?"

Gary took a step back. "You need a little time to think it over. No problem. Why don't you just give us a buzz in the morning? Not too early." Gary dropped onto the couch and pulled a beer out of the Styrofoam cooler next to the barbecue chicken mop bucket.

"Thanks. We will." I dug my fingers into Brooks's arm and dragged him out of the room.

"Where did you find these guys?" I asked the minute the door clicked behind me.

"They work at this sushi place. I was standing outside having a smoke when they popped out to join me during their break."

"They're smokers, then?"

"No, they chew."

I breathed deeply through my nose. "Of course they do." I eyed the McDonald's across the street. "I'm not sure I can live in a place without a bathroom."

"You'd have to if we were living in my car."

My fingers curled into my palms. "Is this really the best you think we can do?"

Brooks shrugged. "I don't know. But it sort of fell into my lap and I kind of figured sometimes the universe gives you a gift." He rubbed his hands over my shoulders. "They seem like okay guys."

"They used the word 'stoked.'"

His boy grin emerged and my face warmed. "Yeah, but they work at a sushi place. Bet they bring home lots of good food."

"Let's hope it's better than chicken out of a mop bucket."

Brooks looped his fingers through mine. "They're harmless. And it's a room that doesn't cost eighty-nine dollars a night."

I looked back at the door to the apartment and sighed. "Okay, we can give it a try."

"You don't want to go back in and check out the room? Gary told me there's a mattress already in there for us to sleep on. I guess their old roommate left it behind."

"Hmm . . . maybe we can pick up our own futon. I'm not trying to be a diva, but I'm not really into the idea of bed bugs."

Brooks steered me toward his car. "Okay, princess, we'll pick up a futon."

I slipped into the car and pulled my phone out of my pocket. I slid the temporary SIM card Brooks had gotten me into the back and texted Ali.

Gannon: *Found a job. Found a place.*

Ali: *Already? Did Brooks find 1?*

I peeked at him fiddling with the radio.

Gannon: *Not yet. But he will soon.*

Ali: *If u say so. Miss u.*

A lump blocked the back of my throat.

Gannon: *Me 2. Say hi to Jace.*

Ali: *Ok. Want me 2 say anything 2 ur mom?*

I stared at the phone screen too long.

Gannon: *No.*

My phone was back in my bag before I could change my mind. I gave Brooks a too-bright smile and pulled out the menthol cigarettes in the glove compartment. Brooks shook his head and started the car.

21

My life became a series of odd-hour shifts at the pizza place, after which I returned to the bizarre scheming and crazy shenanigans of Gary and Bruce. When I walked in the door at night, Brooks quizzed me on whether anything suspicious had happened. Did strange people ask me questions? Did anyone take too much of an interest in me? He was alone too much. He grew increasingly depressed and paranoid as he was turned down for job after job. Even the shitty ones. He complained all the illegal aliens were taking the jobs. I worried about him and stayed up too late talking with him, filling him with me so he wasn't left with the growing fear of his father finding him or the memories of whatever happened in juvie.

"Why won't you tell me about it?" I asked one night, playing with the new blue in his hair. I'd spent the night bleaching and re-dyeing him, no easy task considering I'd had to sneak buckets of water out of the McDonald's. Gary and Bruce got drunk and dyed their chest hair blue "in solidarity," whatever that meant.

"Juvie doesn't matter. It doesn't mean anything other than my time away from you."

He laced his fingers in mine and put them over the tattoo on his chest.

"All that therapy in the hospital was bullshit. But there was something about just saying things out loud that made it sort of better."

"Well, juvie sure wasn't hospital therapy." The bitterness in his tone lashed out at me. He took a deep breath and squeezed my fingers. "We've talked about this before. I'm not inviting you into my crap salad. This. Here. Now. It's all that matters."

My heart pounded. I felt that way too sometimes, but when I got close to it, near enough to poke it with a stick and examine it, the feeling overwhelmed me with fear.

I licked my way up his stomach to the Gannon bleeding-heart tattoo. My tongue traced over it and I ached for something I didn't know how to explain.

"You want something," he said, somehow invading my thoughts.

I shook my head.

"You do. You just don't know how to tell me yet."

I opened my mouth, but before I could answer, the door

to our room flung open. Gary stood in a towel and flannel shirt.

"Brooks. We're going to do the Polar Bear Club in the Mississippi River. Grab a towel and let's roll."

Brooks tried to sit up, but my hand pushed him back down. I wrapped the blanket tighter around myself, wary of Gary seeing me even in a tank top and pajama shorts.

"The Polar Bear Club is in January," I said.

"No. They do it like every month in Minnesota. This guy at the sushi place told me about it. It has something to do with this Swedish thing. You submerge yourself in the Mississippi and then you sit in a hot sauna until you're completely fried. And then you go back in the Mississippi again. You see how many times you can do it before passing out."

I arched a brow at him. "And this is fun to you?"

"Hell, yeah!" he shouted. A sound of a flowing stream came from the living room behind Gary. I peeked past him and saw Bruce peeing in the yellow chicken bucket. Classy. He pulled his trunks up and popped his head in.

"Brooks, my man, are you coming?" Bruce had on an I SEE DUMB PEOPLE T-shirt that stretched too tight across his beer belly. His hairy legs peeked out from his long bathing-suit trunks and snow boots.

"No," I said at the same time Brooks said, "Yeah."

I shook my head. "This isn't October at the pool. It's late March in Minnesota. You'll freeze."

Bruce flapped his hands at me. "No. Dude, didn't you hear what Gary said about the sauna? Hot, cold, hot, cold, hot, cold. It's totally good for you."

Gary bounced on his feet next to Bruce, nodding his head.

"You all are lunatics. Brooks stays here."

Brooks sat up and I quickly snatched the blanket to my chest.

"I love you, sweetheart, but I'm going. I need something like this."

He dropped a kiss on my speechless mouth and rifled through his duffel bag for a towel. My eyes widened. He was really doing this?

Before I could move, jump up, and forcibly tie him to the bed, he was out the door with Gary and Bruce. Laughter circled them, and a tiny piece inside me cracked off.

Instead of sitting in our too-quiet apartment, waiting for the guys to get back, I went to the Pizza by the Slice. It was the only place I could think of. No one really talked to me there, except the customers. I didn't know Spanish, and every other employee spoke it all the time. The manager ignored me except to hand me money at the end of the week and tell me to move faster when I got slices for people.

I ordered a piece of cheese pizza and retreated to a corner table. I picked the cheese off my slice and rolled it into a ball on the edge of my plate. After two weeks of working at the

Pizza by the Slice and eating for free, my face had broken out from the grease. Now I stuck to the boxed salads and the pizza dough. And tried not to think about my brothers maybe eating the same thing.

A woman in a brown sweater and long corduroy skirt walked in. I'd seen her a few times. She was quiet. Probably about thirty years old. Ate her slice alone and read books at one of the tables by the window. Her hair was pulled back in a tight bun, but her face was clear and free of tension. Her eyes scanned the restaurant after she ordered, and with her plate in her hand she walked toward me.

"Can I join you?"

I blinked at her. Didn't she see the fifteen empty tables around me? "Why?"

"I don't feel like eating alone," she said, and sat down across from me.

I shrugged. Evidently, my feelings on the matter weren't important.

"You work here, right?" she asked, cutting her slice with a plastic fork and knife.

I nodded.

"Are you in school?"

A blush reached my cheeks before I could tamp it down. "No."

"How old are you?"

"How old are you?" I snapped back.

"Thirty-two," she said with a smile.

I didn't say anything, so she took a few bites of pizza. I rolled the ball of cheese around my plate.

"You seem young," she said at last. "Are you at the U?"

"Hardly," I snorted.

"How old are you?" she asked again.

I lifted my chin. "Eighteen."

"Oh. Do you live around here?"

I raised a shoulder. Why was this random woman prying into my life? Caution licked at me from the inside but warred with a desperate need to connect with somebody. Anybody.

"Well, I do," she said. "I've seen you walking to work. I'm not trying to pry. Just making conversation."

The spring inside me released. I was being too cagey. "Sorry. I'm not used to people being interested in me."

"Really?" Her eyebrows shot up and she studied me more closely. "Not even your parents?"

I barked out a laugh. "No. Definitely not them."

"Don't they ask about your day when you get home?"

Guilt burned in the back of my throat. "I don't live with them," I mumbled.

"Oh. Do you live by yourself?"

"Do you live by yourself?" I fired back. She may have been trying to be nice, but Brooks's paranoia had seeped into me.

"Yeah. I do. I work at the library."

I laughed and she tilted her head. "Sorry," I said. "Just with the bun and everything, it's kind of cliché."

She smiled. "Yeah. And now I'm the lonely spinster talking to random strangers in the pizza place."

"Yeah. Something like that," I answered.

She took another bite of pizza. "I just felt like talking to someone tonight and my friends aren't around."

"Oh. Okay. Umm . . . I live with my boyfriend and a couple of roommates."

I wanted so much for this to be normal, but as soon as I said "boyfriend" I felt like I'd said too much. I pushed out of my seat before she could ask me any more questions. I snatched my plate and dumped it into the trash.

"I gotta go," I stammered. "I'll see you."

She nodded and pursed her lips. The door swung open wide and I bolted outside, pushing the incoming delivery guy out of the way.

On the way home I thought about calling Ali. I missed her more than I'd thought I could. I wanted to talk to her, tell her everything, spill everything so that I didn't feel so incredibly alone. But I couldn't. For Brooks or for myself. Ali was too connected to my old life. I needed someone else. But I couldn't entertain the possibility of a new friend. Not with how things were with Brooks and me. My life, my future belonged to him.

. . .

"Where were you?" Brooks asked as soon as I took a step into the living room. He snatched my hand and pulled me into our room, slamming the door behind us.

I crossed my arms. "Why do you care? If I don't have any say in you throwing yourself into the Mississippi, you certainly don't have any say in what the hell I do."

He flinched. "I came back," he said, his voice dropping. "I felt bad and I came back. And you weren't here." His face was too raw, too vulnerable, too un-Brooks. "I was worried."

I stepped toward him and he pulled me into his arms. "Sorry," I whispered.

"Don't make me go through that again. I thought something happened to you. Then I thought you'd left me."

"Silly boy." I tugged on his hair. "I love you."

"I can't lose you. Do you understand?" The intensity of him stole my breath.

I nodded.

He lifted my chin and stared hard at me. "Do you understand?"

"Yes," I whispered.

"I got you a gift," he said, releasing me and picking up a brown bag next to his duffel bag. "I know you're missing something. You won't tell me, but I can see it. We can get it back." His hand slipped into the bag and he pulled out a small envelope. He shook it and two tabs of E slipped into his hand.

I gasped. Part of me wanted to snatch them from his fingers and take them both myself, get back that feeling of everything being possible, and the other part wanted to throw them out the window and draw everything I ached for out of Brooks. The boy who'd turned my life upside down and wouldn't help me right it. I was too paralyzed to move, straddled on the line of a decision I didn't know how to make.

"I thought you said this wasn't a good idea for me." My voice shook.

"But you liked it, right? It made you feel good. You need it. I can tell." He pressed one of the tabs into my open hand and I stared. "Let's do this together."

Tears blurred my vision. "I can't," I whispered. "I want it so much, but it's not right. It's not what I'm missing. I'll just want more."

He took the pill from my hand and dropped both pills back into the envelope before skimming his fingers over my tears. "Then what is it? What can I do?" Pleading desperation. God, why couldn't I fix this? Fix him? Fix me?

My knees crumpled and I curled onto the bed. I had no answer. Not anything I understood or could explain. All I had was the truth of the moment. "Love me."

So he did.

22

A week later I walked in from work to a hillbilly chemistry lab. Gary and Bruce had gloves and lab goggles on. I could see the bright blue chest hair through their white T-shirts. Brooks sat smoking on the couch.

"What's up?"

"Did anyone follow you?" he asked, looking me up and down.

My shirt was covered in pizza sauce and my hair was droopy. I'd run out of the detangler I used in place of actually washing my hair every day, and it didn't seem in the budget to replace it. I'd started eating only twice a day, once at the Pizza by the Slice and once with Brooks in the morning. We spent our money on rent, cigarettes, and condoms. Brooks had lost so much weight I suspected he wasn't eating anything aside from the bagel sandwiches we got in the mornings or whatever suspicious-looking leftover sushi Gary and Bruce brought home.

"No one followed me. No one asked questions. No one said anything in English to me all day, other than 'Give me a slice.'"

He tugged me onto the couch beside him and kissed my forehead. "Poor baby." His hands moved to massage my neck and I melted into him, watching the crazy around us.

"What are you two up to?" I asked.

Gary lifted his goggles. "We're making moonshine."

I laughed. "You're shitting me."

Bruce grinned and I noticed he had something green in his teeth. "No. I found a recipe on the Internet."

"Do we suddenly have a computer?" I asked. Of course we didn't. We didn't have running water. I had to bathe in the sink at work or at the McDonald's, a sort of sponge bath like they'd done for me at the hospital. I was convinced my manager thought I was homeless, which I might as well have been for the number of times I'd brushed my teeth in a bathroom riddled with graffiti. Gary and Bruce had worked out some sort of agreement with the McDonald's manager that involved providing him with dime bags of weed once a week for no questions asked. When I snuck in the back entrance every morning and night, I kept my head down and tried not to draw attention to the fact that I never bought food there.

"There's a computer at work," Bruce said, completely missing my sarcasm. "Gary, hand me that funnel." The two of them started to bicker over the directions. Then they disappeared into their room with a large glass jug.

Brooks's fingers played on the base of my spine and I sighed. "Rough day, sweetheart?" he whispered into my ear.

"Something like that. What about you? Any luck on the job front?"

Brooks tensed. I shouldn't have pushed it. I knew he was discouraged over the whole thing. I'd stopped asking him after the first few weeks, but we'd been with Gary and Bruce for over a month and I didn't know how much longer I could hole up with them.

"No," he said. "But I talked to Kenji again. He said a guy was nosing around asking questions. I'm sure it was my dad."

I leaned forward, turned and looked at him. "Really?"

Annoyance flashed across his face. "I told you he was determined. That's why you always need to be careful about who you talk to. He won't let me walk away without trying to find me."

"Couldn't it have been your probation officer?"

"I'm sure it was my dad."

I opened my mouth to argue, but Brooks held his hand up.

"It doesn't matter. I won't let him get near us. Kenji won't tell him anything."

Somehow trusting a drug dealer didn't feel quite as reassuring to me as it obviously did to Brooks. But I also couldn't quite wrap my head around the idea that Brooks's dad was coming for him.

"Kenji's friend out here still needs help," Brooks continued.

So he was going to deal? I wanted to tell him not to—it couldn't lead to anything good—but the thought of the two of us being able to live in a place with a kitchen and bathroom was like a dangling carrot to a rabbit.

"Let's give it a few more weeks," I said.

"The opportunity may not be around in a few weeks."

I wrapped his hands around my waist so I could sink into his chest, smell his Indian Spirit cloud. "If it's the right thing to do, it will be."

He nuzzled into my neck. "Whatever you say, sweetheart."

The bitter edge in Brooks's voice showed itself more and more often. He didn't like that I had to work. He detested the fact that he couldn't get a job. He couldn't stand that there was something wrong with me that neither of us seemed to know how to fix. And I couldn't tell him that I wasn't the only one obviously broken.

"I'm gonna call Ali," I said, standing up from the couch.

Brooks's mouth turned down. "Why?"

"She's my best friend. I told her I'd check in. I barely call her as it is."

He raised a shoulder. "She's not part of our life."

I bit my bottom lip. Did that mean I couldn't still be friends with her? Resentment pooled into the empty spaces of my brain.

"Are you using the new phone I got you?"

I nodded. Brooks had been providing me with new unlocked phones of a suspicious origin after every call I made to Ali. He didn't even trust just switching SIM cards in my old phone anymore.

"Okay, give it to me when you're done; I'll pick up a new one tomorrow."

I didn't say anything else, just turned and retreated into our room, plunking myself on the bed.

"It's about frickin' time," Ali said as soon as she picked up the phone. "You texted you'd call at nine. It's ten thirty."

"Sorry. Work."

"Why do you keep having to change phone numbers every month? It's ridiculous and seems sketchy and totally paranoid. I mean, seriously, who the hell are you running from? You're both eighteen. The two of you are acting like Bonnie and Clyde."

I swallowed. "Well, Brooks is in violation of his probation. And he's also worried about his dad tracking him." I hated that I had to defend him and hated even more that a little part of me knew she was right.

"You should call home," she said, and her voice caught.

"What's wrong?"

She took a deep breath. "Your dad split. Moved into his own place. Your mom's on her own with the boys."

Guilt and anger wrestled inside me. My skin itched. I took three long breaths. "How's she doing?"

"How the hell do you think she's doing? She's lost two family members in the past two months. She's the only guard left alone with the inmates running the prison. She's a hot mess."

Fury sliced through me. "Why are you putting this on me?"

"I'm not, but Gannon, for Christ's sake, have a little compassion. She sucks as a mom, but she's still *your* mom."

My hands were trembling. I looked around the room for Brooks's brown paper bag. This could all be so much better with E. "What am I supposed to do?"

"Call her. Just call her. She wants to hear your voice."

I didn't say anything and finally Ali sighed and hung up. My eyes fell on the paper bag and I shook it until the envelope with the E dropped out. I opened it and peered at the white pills. My thumb moved across the envelope and a tiny drop of blood appeared. Relief. From a paper cut. Jesus. The door swung open and my hand slipped beneath my legs. Brooks took two strides into the room, slamming the door behind him.

He yanked my hand out and the envelope dropped to the floor. "What did I tell you?"

I couldn't speak. My world spun in a fuzzy blur like I'd been drinking.

"We do this together. We do everything together," he said, and picked up the envelope.

I stood up, my head still spinning. "I have to get out of here." He followed me. I put my hand up and shoved him back. "Alone."

The hurt that flashed across his face was nothing in comparison to the overwhelming urge to flee. I pushed my way out of the apartment, ignoring Gary and Bruce's puzzled expressions as I left. The cold night air filled my lungs and soothed the itchiness of my skin. Breathe in, breathe out. I floated over the sidewalk, unaware of anything but the air in my lungs and the buzzing in my head.

My feet carried me to the Pizza by the Slice. I had no idea why, but then I saw the woman who'd sat down with me at a table by the window, nibbling on her pizza. Her brows furrowed when she saw me. She pointed to the seat across from her. I shook my head, but my body steered me inside anyway. I dropped into the seat and stared at my hands. The blood on my thumb was smeared and dried.

"Why are you always here?" I blurted out.

"I live across the street. I'm not always here. But I'm not a great cook. Chinese takeout gets old. I guess pizza does too." She pushed her plate away.

235

"I'm Amelia," I said. It was stupid, a pull to something I couldn't have, but I couldn't stop myself.

"It's nice to meet you."

"It wasn't supposed to be like this."

She gave me a warm encouraging smile. "What are we talking about?"

"My life. It wasn't supposed to be like this. It's not like I expected everything to be perfect. We're teenagers without high school diplomas, trying to live together. I've seen enough of those reality shows to realize it isn't exactly a recipe for success. I just didn't think I would miss everything so much."

I brushed away tears and she handed me a napkin to blow my nose.

"Thanks."

"No problem," she said. "Why don't you go home?" Her voice was so calm and nonjudgmental. I wanted to tell her the rest. I wanted to pour everything I was feeling out onto the table in front of this stranger.

The glass banged next to my head and I looked into Brooks's devastated eyes. The urge to spill my life to this woman whooshed out of me and I was out of my chair, stumbling for the door without saying good-bye.

"Amelia," she called out as my hand hauled the door open. "I'm Grace Miller. I'm on the third floor across the street. Come find me if you ever need to talk."

I blinked. What the hell was I doing? I shook my head, exited the restaurant, and walked straight into Brooks's arms. He held me too tight and we were both shaking from all the things that weren't being said, trying to press our emotions into each other. Squeezing each other so hard, like that would somehow mold us back together. I pulled away from him and searched his face. Some of the anxiety had eased, but the question was still there. The question I couldn't answer.

I gnawed my lip, slipped my hand into his, and led him to the park around the corner.

"You have to tell me. Who was that woman? You know her? What'd you say to her?" he asked, half a block down the street.

"Nothing. I don't know her. She lives across the street and eats here sometimes."

"Why were you talking to her?"

"I don't know. She's no one. But I have no one to talk to."

He looked at me like I'd slapped him. "You have me."

I touched his cheek and kissed him. "I have you."

He peered into my face. "What's going on with you?" Again with this. Always the same question. Always my nonanswers.

I barely scraped out the energy to say, "Nothing."

We sat on a bench. Coldness seeped into my jeans and I snuggled closer to him. I stared at a couple walking with their arms hooked together. The man was in a fancy long coat over a suit. The woman wore leather boots, a peacoat, and a matching hat and scarf. Married maybe. In love for sure.

"Do you think that'll be us one day?" I asked.

"You mean me with my corporate job and you meeting me after work where you're a hygienist or some shit?"

We looked at each other and laughed. "Yeah. Didn't think so."

Brooks steepled my hand with his. "I want that for us, baby. Well, not that exactly, because fuck if you'll ever catch me in that asshole coat." He chuckled. "But a life like that. Where we aren't running from anyone. Where we have jobs and can just be together as we are. Maybe even have kids one day."

I bit my tongue, swallowed past the dryness in my throat, and squeezed his hand. "I want that too."

"I promise it'll be better. Soon. I love you."

"I love you too."

He pulled me closer and dropped kisses on my cheeks and forehead, like he had the first time we were in the woods together. Then he hooked his arm through mine and we walked home. We didn't speak. Nothing was resolved, but at least the itchiness had subsided a little. I flipped off the lights in our room, tangled myself up in him, and ignored the fear circling around my head.

23

Brooks started dealing. It was sort of inevitable. The paranoia and bitterness around him was infecting everything, and in the end I told him to call Kenji's friend. I was terrified, but hoped that making money of his own would change the silence between us. My heart flipped the first day he came back with his boy grin and a handful of twenties.

He pulled off my boots and started kissing my feet.

"Gross," I said, kicking him off me. "I've been wearing those boots all day."

He licked my ankle. "I don't care."

And the thing was, he didn't. I folded my feet underneath me. "Kiss something else."

He leered at me and I swatted him. "That's not what I meant."

He pulled my shirt off and flipped me on my stomach onto our futon. "Your back is beautiful," he whispered, kissing a path down my spine. "No scars. No marks. Just a gorgeous canvas."

I turned my head to the side so I could see him better. "Yeah, I'm surprised the fire didn't get me there, but I guess you pulled me out before it could."

He smiled. "Guess so." His finger figure-eighted down my spinal column. "You should get a tattoo."

"Not in the budget," I said.

"Might be now," he said, and winked at me. Was it wrong that I was so glad about his drug-dealing euphoria? Over him finally, finally being a little happy, as if it could somehow turn me right side up?

"We need to get out of here first. I don't know how much more I can take of dashing across the street to pee and eating crappy food every night. I can cook, you know."

His fingers kneaded. "I didn't know. But I'm glad to hear it. Even I'm starting to get sick of leftover sushi."

I nodded. "Plus, I'm not exactly sure how safe it is to eat food that comes from the hands of Gary and Bruce."

Brooks laughed. "It's gonna be okay. Things will be better with us now. I promise."

The truth slipped past his lips and pressed against the inside of my chest. Things had been getting worse every day. Not just with the apartment, but with us. He knew it too. The dream of jobs and security and kids was not in our cards. We lived minute by minute, holding on to drops of water that evaporated before we could lick them up. There was no break for Junior Mints and horror movies, just a pounding grind and a seemingly bottomless pit.

He reached across the futon and dug around in a take-out bag still sitting there. We never cleaned anything. Too exhausted to bother, too dirty ourselves to care much about the state of our room. My head lifted as he shook the bag.

"What are you doing?"

"Trying to make things better. You trust me, right?"

I took three deep breaths. "Yes."

"Good. Now head down." I pressed my face into the pillow and waited. Paper tore. I looked up again.

"What . . . ?"

"No peeking. Head down."

Then I felt it. The press of something against my back. "Is that a chopstick?" I asked into the pillow.

"Yeah. I'm going to draw you a tattoo." He pressed harder and the cheap wood scraped against my skin.

My heart beat faster and I wiggled. He pressed harder still, and a long breath escaped my lips. He rubbed over and over the same area. I didn't have the first clue what he was drawing, but I didn't think he did either. That wasn't the point.

He pulled something else from the takeout bag and I heard

rustling. Then the prongs of a plastic fork bit into the same area he'd just used the chopstick on. My body shook and he went over the area again. I ached to see it, ask for more, something harder, but I gathered myself inside and shut it all off.

"Enough," I said, and he dropped the fork to the floor.

"Are you sure?" he whispered, pressing kisses between my shoulder blades and down the path of the newly scraped skin.

I nodded and slipped my shirt back on. I was tempted to take it off again, wanting to re-create the day in the storage garage when everything came out and Brooks and I connected like we never had before. But I also knew now more than ever it would change things for us. Unglue the already cracking pieces of our relationship.

"Okay," he said, and grabbed the other chopstick, rubbing the two together at a weird angle until the tips were rough and splintery. He pressed one into my hand. He pulled off his shirt and lay down on his back beside me. "Do me."

"What?"

"Draw me a tattoo, Gannon. Right here, underneath yours." Underneath mine. My name carved into him forever.

I shook my head. "No. I'm not any good at drawing."

He stared at me. "I don't care." He wrapped his hand around mine and pushed the chopstick against the pale skin beneath his other tattoo. I tried to ease my hand up, but he wouldn't let me.

"I don't want to hurt you."

His gaze didn't break from mine, but he pushed my hand down more. "It's okay."

It was a chopstick. Nothing really. A piece of wood with a slightly rough edge, but his whole body strummed like he was asking for something else. Almost like the day with the belt, only different, more dark and dangerous. This wasn't about me. It was about something I couldn't quite wrap my head around.

"I *won't* hurt you."

"Please, baby."

I nearly buckled at the tone in his voice. He'd given me so much of himself; how could I not give him this?

"Why? Why do you want this?"

"I deserve it," he whispered.

Tears pushed from my eyes and trailed down my cheeks. The space between us was too wide. Too deep. "You don't," I choked out. "You don't deserve to be hurt."

I reached out and touched the wetness on his face. His tears. My tears. It was all too much. My heart collapsed. He pulled me toward him and curled in to my chest, letting me hold him like a small child. I smoothed my hand over his hair.

"What happened to you?" I said.

"The things I did in juvie. The things they made me do. I deserve for you to hurt me. I just wanted to get back to you." His words stumbled and stuttered, dropping from his mouth in a strange and low voice. "It was the only thing that kept me going. I would do anything to get back to you. I tried not to be noticed. To keep my head down and just do my time. But they found me. It was like they knew how desperate I was to get out. And they made me choke on it."

"What are you talking about? What does that mean?" Questions tumbled from my lips along with the desperate desire to know how broken he really was. How broken we were.

He ran his fingers over my palms. "Your hands are so soft," he said as if he hadn't heard my questions. "So gentle. Your body responds to me and it isn't in anger or hatred or anything beyond just loving me. It's not like that for the guys in juvie. The first time I went in, I was too young and not worth their time. But this time they knew. They shoved me to my knees and told me not to fight. Fighting would just add time to my stay. So I took it. I took it all and I thought of you. I thought only of getting back to you."

A sob escaped my lips and he finally looked at me. The hole in my heart was large enough for him to climb inside. I wanted him to. I wanted him to feel safe. Guilt at what had been done to him because of my parents' decision pricked along my skin. I kicked the chopstick across the room with my bare foot. I moved my hands over him and prayed my touch could take it all away.

"I love you," I whispered.

He scrubbed his hand over his face and a tiny smile pulled at his mouth. "I know."

The door flew open and Gary and Bruce bounded in and dropped onto our bed.

"Guys. *Night of the Comet* is playing at the Riverside Theater. That's like a zombie cult classic. You have to come see it with us."

I stared at Brooks. He slipped his shirt on and swiped at his face, and the cold, guarded look returned. "We need a lock on our door," I told him. "I'm installing one tomorrow."

Bruce scoffed. "Give me a break. We've seen way better than anything you've got to offer." Brooks growled, but Bruce ignored him. "Gary's got a porn app on his phone. You're a scrawny chick with no tits. I'd have more luck getting off imagining Gary's mom."

"Dude, I told you to stop talking shit about my mom."

Bruce shrugged. "What can I say? She totally got hot after she had all that work done."

Gary slugged him and looked back at Brooks and me. "So, *Night of the Comet*, it's not exactly eighties horror, but pretty close. You guys in? We could barbecue some chicken afterwards."

"Let's hope they're not using the mop bucket," I mumbled to Brooks.

"Urine's sterile," Bruce said. "And we cleaned that bucket with bleach yesterday."

"By all means, then, put your chicken in it. Barbecue and

bleach sounds like a really appetizing combination." God, I was living in a petri dish. It was amazing I hadn't gotten an infection on my leg burns.

Brooks pulled out two twenty-dollar bills and handed them to Gary. "Tell you what. You guys head over to the theater and buy us all tickets and we'll meet you out front."

Gary pocketed the bills and bounced up and down like a toddler. "Okay. But don't be late. The movie starts in like twenty minutes and I hate to miss previews."

Brooks ushered them out the door, then went to the closet to rifle through some plastic bags he'd stashed there. Bags I wanted to look in, but I stopped myself every time I grew curious. Brooks's business. If he wanted me to know . . .

"What are you doing?"

He turned back to me and held out a bottle of Elmer's glue. "Those guys are assholes to you. I'm not letting them get away with that shit."

"So you're gonna glue 'em."

Brooks grinned. Old Brooks. My face cracked into a matching grin. I loved this boy.

"No. I thought of this the other day when they were mouthing off about your hair on the way to the Polar Bear thing."

I raised an eyebrow. "The guys who blued their chests had something to say about my hair?"

Brooks nodded, then walked out of the room. He returned

with a bottle of moisturizer. "Gary and Bruce's masturbation lotion. The other night when they were totally wasted, they went off on what a quality product it was."

He unscrewed the glue and dumped it into the moisturizer.

I giggled and he winked at me. Then he screwed the cap back on and returned it to the guys' room. "So are we good?"

It was a loaded question on so many levels, but from the look on his face I knew what he needed me to say. "Of course. It's you and me against the world, baby."

He held out his hand and led me out of the room.

24

A week passed before I broke down and called Mom. I only saw Grace Miller once during that time, and I couldn't even meet her eyes when I handed her a slice of pizza. Brooks was gone from the apartment almost all the time. I was glad he was getting out, but I hated the reason for it and hated the risk he was taking.

After a particularly horrible day when the only words I said to anyone were "Do you want something to drink with that?" and "Restrooms are for paying customers only," I found myself staring at my phone, sliding my fingers over the digits of Mom's number. I dialed before I could change my mind.

"Hello." Her voice was just the same, and I was struck by

the compulsion to fall asleep to the sound of her singing like I did when I was a little girl.

"It's me."

"Amelia. Oh thank God. How are you? Where are you? Come home."

I blinked back tears. "I'm fine. I'm not coming home."

"Where are you?" I could hear one of the boys' video games in the background and celebratory shouting.

"What is that?"

"Miguel beat some game, I think." She released a sigh. "You're not going to tell me where you are."

"It's probably better not to."

"Better for who? Michael? Why should I care about what's better for him? Is he there? Put him on the phone. I want to say something to him."

"Mom. Don't do this. He's not here, but even if he were, I wouldn't let you say anything to him. You have no idea what you did to him by sending him to juvie." I pulled a filtered menthol from the box and lit it.

"Dad left," she said in a detached voice.

"I heard. How are you?"

"Okay." She released another sigh. "He sees the boys on the weekend. Takes them out for too much sugar and then brings them home for me to deal with."

I didn't respond. I couldn't offer anything that would do her any good.

"Will you please come home?" she whispered. I nearly broke in two.

"I can't. It wouldn't help anyway. I'd just be one more thing for you to deal with."

"That's not true," she said. "You were always a big help with the boys."

I blew out a stream of smoke. "Sure I was."

"Please come home," she said again. "We're a family. I'm your mother. I'll always be your mother. They'll always be your brothers. Please, please come home."

"No." I stubbed out my cigarette. "I love you, Mom."

"Amelia, don't go."

I clicked the phone off and curled into a ball on our futon. Tears dampened our blanket and I didn't do anything to stop them. Just stayed that way until Brooks walked in smelling of pot and slipped his arms around me.

"Do you want to talk about it?" he whispered, massaging my shoulders.

"No," I said, shaking his hands off me. A massage wasn't going to make this go away. And he'd be mad if he found out I'd called my mom.

He pulled me in to him, and before long I heard the soft sounds of his snoring. I slid out from under his arm and tiptoed across the room. I scrawled a note on the back of a Pizza by the Slice menu and propped it on the coat I'd made him get from Goodwill. *Be right back. Going to get some food.*

My feet led me back toward work, and before I was fully aware of it, I was standing in front of the building across the street. Grace Miller's building. It used to be a three-flat, but then the basement had been converted to a seamstress's and the first floor was a small expensive coffee shop. The one time I'd been in the coffee shop, the chatty barista mentioned the top floor was still an apartment.

I scanned the business names outside the door, then saw hers. Grace Miller. My hand hovered over the buzzer next to her name. I took a step back from the building and stumbled. I caught myself and spun around. Four steps down and I heard the door swing open.

"Amelia." Her voice was a question and an offer all in one. My feet slowed.

"Yeah?"

"Did you come to see me?"

I shook my head.

"What are you doing here?" She stepped closer to me.

I shook my head again.

Her hand touched my shoulder. "Is everything all right?"

"I used to cut." The words burst from my mouth before I could swallow them back. "I don't anymore, but I used to. Then

I went to the hospital and stopped." She steered me to the steps and sat down. I liked how she didn't care about dirt on her pants or that she might be blocking other people from getting in.

"When did you get out of the hospital?"

I shrugged and sat down beside her. The steps were cold and I shivered a bit. "A few months ago."

She nodded.

My body itched and tingled. I rose and walked in a small circle two times to calm myself down. "The thing is, I miss it."

"Cutting?"

"Yeah."

"Maybe you should talk to someone. Are you still in contact with your doctor at the hospital?"

I squeezed a breath in. "No. And I don't want to cut anymore. I miss it, but I don't want to do it."

"Amelia, I want to help you. But I don't think I'm the right person . . ."

"Brooks helps me. He tries. But beneath everything, beneath how much I love him, the ache is still there. And I don't know how to make it go away."

Silence. Nothing between us but Grace Miller's penetrating stare.

"Brooks loves me," I said.

She stood up, smoothed the light coat she wore, and dusted

her khaki pants. "Okay. But maybe he isn't the right person to help you either."

I didn't speak. I didn't have to. I knew what she meant. What she thought. Judgment pelted me from every side.

"Forget I said anything." I spun on my heel. I glanced back as I walked away. She stood with her arms crossed, staring at her feet and shaking her head. What the hell had I been thinking to talk to this strange woman? She didn't get anything about my life. I was an idiot for even trying.

25

The next day I sat on the couch, watching Gary and Bruce play a game involving a twenty-sided die and a glass bong. There appeared to be no rules other than to take a bong hit every time you rolled more than a three.

"Dudes," Bruce said, "we gotta have a party."

I eyed the ten-by-ten living room. "In here?"

Bruce grinned and took another bong hit. "Totally."

"We could have a moonshine party. The guys at work wanna try our home brew," Gary said.

"I thought that didn't work out so well last time." Not that it hadn't been hilarious to see Gary and Bruce blowing chunks all night. There was evidently no end to the uses of the yellow mop bucket.

"It was our freshman effort. I guess we were supposed to

wait two weeks to let it ferment before drinking, not two days. I must've copied it down wrong. My bad." Bruce gave Gary a "no hard feelings" fist bump.

"I think you guys should wait for warmer weather for a party," I said.

Gary rubbed his five o'clock shadow. "Nah. We should have it next weekend. But you gotta invite some of your girl-friends over since we mostly just know guys."

I started to tell them I didn't know any girls, but then thought better of it. With any luck they'd forget about the party idea after half a dozen more bong hits and a night of watching bad porn on Gary's phone. And maybe, just maybe, Brooks and I wouldn't even be around for it if they did remember.

Brooks walked in on the tail end of an argument over whether Gary and Bruce should make fondue on hot plates for the party. He was carrying a plastic bag and wore a giant grin on his face. He nodded hello to the guys and motioned me toward our room.

"You look happy," I said, sliding my arms around him.

He kissed my nose. "I am."

"Did you find us our own place?"

"No. But we're close. A few more deals and I'll probably have enough saved for the security deposit on a studio."

I slid my hands beneath his black T-shirt. "Why the grin, then?"

He held the plastic bag up. "I got you another present."

"Really?"

"Yes. This is just part of it. The rest will come tomorrow."

I snatched the bag from him and opened it. "A jigsaw?"

He grinned. "Yeah. I know you've been missing working with your tools. I met a guy at the Home Depot who said I could take some of their scrap wood. I'm gonna pick it up in the morning. I'll get a hammer and nails and wood glue, too."

I swallowed twice. The jigsaw reminded me so much of Dennis I had to bite the inside of my cheek not to cry. "Thank you. I love it."

I put the bag down and wrapped my arms around him.

Brooks smiled again. "I knew you would. I told you I'd make things better."

I kissed him and pulled him onto the bed. "Did you remember to pick me up a cell phone?" I whispered.

He stopped kissing me. "Aw, crap, sorry, baby, I forgot."

"But you tossed my other one and you told me you'd get a new one today."

"I know," he said and sat up. "But I had a lot of shit to take care of. I forgot."

I rolled over and pulled the scratchy orange blanket on top of me.

He tugged at it. "Don't be like that. It's not that big of a

deal. What do you even need a cell phone for? We have mine."
He reached for me and I shoved him off.

"Because I want to be able to call you in an emergency."

He combed his fingers through his hair. "I'm sorry. You're right. I don't want you left without a way to reach me."

"I hate how we have to keep switching phones. I can never remember all these numbers. No one can ever get a hold of me. It sucks."

He released a breath. "I don't want to risk anyone finding us."

I turned to him. "You're being paranoid and I feel totally cut off."

"Cut off from who?"

I pulled the blanket tighter around me. "Everyone. We live in a craphole with no kitchen, no computer, no bathroom, for Christ's sake. I work at a pizza place and you're a drug dealer. I don't talk to anyone from home except Ali, and even then it's only every few weeks. I didn't expect my life to be like this when I ran away with you."

He snatched the blanket off me. "Well, excuse me if I see things a little different."

"I—"

"I love you." He threw his pillow across the room. "I hate that every day all I do is worry my old man is gonna find us. You think I wanna deal drugs? You think I wanna get caught and sent to jail? Sent to real prison for leaving the state *with you*?

I'm doing it for you. I'm trying to get you a place of our own so you're not such a moody bitch all the time. And I'm doing the best I can to make this better for you when all you do is complain and keep stuff from me."

I opened my mouth but snapped it shut.

"I don't need this shit," he said, and snatched his coat off the floor. "I'm out of here."

He slammed the door open and pounded past Gary and Bruce outside. When the front door clicked behind him, they howled in laughter. Gary popped his head into my room thirty seconds later.

"Lovers' spat?" he said with a stoned grin. "Wanna hit?" He held the glass bong out but I shook my head.

"He'll be back," he said sagely. "No guy walks out on guaranteed nookie for that long."

I flipped him off before burying my head beneath the blanket to cry. Could Brooks really not understand how lonely I was?

When Gary pulled my door shut, I peeked out. The plastic bag with the jigsaw sat discarded in the corner. I slid out of bed and tucked it into the top of our tiny closet. I couldn't think about Dennis or Ricardo or how hard Brooks was trying to fix me. All I could do was count the breaths coming in and out of my lungs until I finally fell asleep.

• • •

I woke the next morning to Brooks's fingers tracing the burn marks on my legs.

"They could fix these, right?"

I raised a shoulder. "Maybe. They'd have to do some sort of skin grafting. I don't know. It might be too late." And it certainly wasn't in our financial future.

"I like them," he said, sliding his hand over the smooth part of the burn. "I'm sorry about last night. I know you feel isolated. I don't want that. But I don't want you hurt, either."

I laced my fingers through his. "I know. I'm sorry too. You're enough for me; I don't need anything else. I just want us to have our own place."

He nodded and reached his hand behind him. He set a cell phone in the space between us. "I'd do anything for you, you know?"

"I know. Me too."

He leaned over and kissed me. "When do you have to work today?"

I smiled. "Not until this afternoon. I'm closing tonight."

He placed the cell phone on the side of the bed. "I have a few appointments, but I might be able to free my schedule for a little while this morning."

My heart thumped. I grinned at him and beckoned him toward me. He grinned back and closed the space between us. A loud bang vibrated the wall next to our bed.

"I told you he wouldn't stay away from guaranteed nookie for long," Gary yelled through the wall.

"See what I mean? We have to get our own place," I whispered to Brooks.

He nodded. "Soon. I promise. Very soon."

"Even if it is with a scrawny chick with no tits," Gary added, louder this time.

"Hey, Gary," Brooks called back. "I'll give you and Bruce fifty bucks and a dime bag of weed if you disappear for the next two hours."

I swatted Brooks. "We need that money." Loud banging and crashing sounded through the walls. Then muffled voices and scrambling feet.

"Not as much as we need two hours without any interruptions from Gary and Bruce."

26

I had an entire day off for the first time in two weeks. My body sank into the pillows and I grinned at the notion of a quiet, boy-free day. Gary and Bruce left early to work the lunch shift and Brooks slipped out of bed at eleven. He dressed quickly, kissed me on the cheek, and promised he'd be back after his appointments.

I got out of bed twenty minutes later, determined not to miss out on any of the coveted solitude of our empty apartment. But the pungent smell of old puke, barbecue chicken, pee, weed and eau de Gary and Bruce was enough to drive me from our place to a nearby Internet café.

I logged on to the computer with the intent of searching for a better job but found a message from Ricardo in my e-mail.

Gannon,

I don't even know if you'll get this, but in case you do, I wanted to tell you that Dennis misses you. I do too, I guess. I'm only gonna be here a few more months before I go to college. Dennis has been a wreck since you ran away. The only thing he cares about is fixing up the apartment above the store. It's sad, but I think he might be getting it ready for you.

I know you're not planning to come back, but could you maybe write him a letter saying good-bye or something? I know it's none of my business, but he feels real bad about how you two left things. He tried to see you in the hospital, but your parents wouldn't let him. I think they somehow blamed him for not telling them something was wrong.

So, I hope you're good and Brooks is treating you right. You probably have a great job and are really happy. But in case you aren't, you can always come back here. I know Dennis would take you back in a second. Standard hasn't been the same since you left.

Ricardo

By my third read-through of Ricardo's e-mail, tears blurred all the words. My chest felt like it was caving in on itself. The cashier came over and offered me a tissue. I blew my nose and stared at my fingers hovering over the keyboard. I composed three different responses and deleted them all. In the end I didn't answer him at all.

I had planned to see *Saw*, but after the emotional overload of Ricardo's e-mail I couldn't muster enough energy to do anything but go home. I pulled the blanket off our bed and wrapped myself in it on the couch. My eyes locked on the front door and I willed Brooks to return. I texted him to see when he would be back, but he didn't respond.

The click of the door woke me from a dark and twisted dream where I didn't pull Luis from the fire in time. I leaped from the couch into Brooks's arms, burying my head into his shoulder.

"Whoa, Gannon," he said. "Guess you missed me."

"It's late. Where have you been?"

He looked like crap. Dark circles under pallid skin, a T-shirt that smelled like cigarettes and body odor. "Working."

He stepped away from me and went into our bedroom. I followed him, desperate to stay connected. Pushing Ricardo's words deep into the back of my mind.

He rustled through the plastic bags at the bottom of our closet and I saw a sandwich bag full of a white substance.

"Is that coke or heroin?"

"Why do you care?" he answered with his back still facing me. I wanted to reach out and touch him. I wanted everything to be different.

"Do you love me?"

He pulled himself around and stared at me. "Of course. Why would you even ask that?"

My fingers started to tingle, pins and needles creeping into my hands. I opened and closed them, hoping to shake it off, but the feeling was coming like a Mack truck without a driver. No stopping.

"Would you do something for me?"

"I would do anything. You know that. I *have* done everything."

A sob escaped my lips. "I know. I know you have."

He stepped into the bubble around me and placed his hands on my hips. "What's this all about?"

"Quit dealing. I want you to quit."

His hands dropped. "No. You think you want that, but you don't. Not really. You need what the money can get us just as much as I do. Probably more."

"What's that supposed to mean?"

He raked his hand through his greasy hair, and the scent of his body odor was even stronger. "We've burned through our savings. We wouldn't be able to afford to stay here without my money, let alone move out. You wouldn't eat. We'd be living in my car. You could barely last seven hours in the car. You don't want that, but I can't give you the life you want unless I do this."

His words lashed at me, but I refused to let it go. Not this time. Not after Ricardo's e-mail. "You could get a different job."

"Gannon. No one is going to hire me. Look at me."

"You didn't even try, did you?" My voice rose. "You didn't even look for a job. You just took the easy out."

"Fuck you. I didn't take the easy out. This . . ." He waved his hand around our room. "This is hardly the easy out. But excuse me if I haven't yet managed a toehold in corporate America. It's a little hard to do that with a juvie record and a target on your back."

"Enough about your dad. He's not coming after you. If he hasn't managed to find you by now, he's not going to. Why are you so paranoid?"

"Shut up. Just fucking shut up. You have no idea what could happen to me. You think your parents wouldn't come after me for kidnapping their daughter and crossing state lines? You think they're not out there right now hunting me down?"

"They're not. I'm eighteen. It was my choice. I left. They know I left."

He shook his head. God, when had he turned into this? His body hummed with tension.

"I've given my whole life for you. And all you've done is complain, withdraw, and now you ask me to quit dealing. I'm not quitting. I'm not going to suffer through you pulling away from me completely because I can't take care of you."

"I never asked you to take care of me." Tears built on my lashes, but I brushed them away.

"Of course you did. You gave me a broken girl covered in scars and scabs and asked me to fix her."

The air squeezed from my lungs. I stood frozen as Brooks moved toward me again, wrapping his arms around me and holding me so tight I coughed.

He eased his grip and moved his mouth to my ear. "I can't quit. I'll lose you if I quit. I know I will. I'm already losing you, but us with no money, living in my car? You'd never stay."

"Brooks . . ." I wanted to tell him he was wrong. I wanted to assure him that it was me and him forever. But a voice inside of me protested loudly enough for me to bite my tongue.

"I'm gonna prove myself to you, Gannon. I swear to God I will make you believe in us again."

I held him tighter and didn't say anything as he pushed me onto the bed and sank into me.

27

He didn't work the next day. Just stayed with me in bed after I called in sick. He pulled out the envelope of E and I popped the tab into my mouth without a word. He grinned and the shadows faded beneath his eyes.

I ran my hands over his skin and everything felt amazing. I had no sense of time or space. Just Brooks and our bodies. He pressed bottles of water into my hand and forced me to drink in between sex.

Gary and Bruce came in, but I was too out of it to care. Brooks covered me up and told them to leave us alone. The tears started about halfway through the night. I couldn't stop them. My body convulsed with heaving sobs, and even Brooks's arms couldn't take away the acute loneliness that swamped me.

"It's okay, baby. You're just coming down," he whispered, pushing my hair out of my face.

"This didn't happen before. It's worse. It's so much worse. I'm so tired, Brooks."

"Go to sleep, baby."

But I couldn't. I worried if I closed my eyes, I wouldn't wake up again. Even more, I worried I'd wake up and find myself face-to-face with the shitty life we'd cobbled together. I wanted the euphoria; I wanted to feel only Brooks. I didn't want the piss bucket and the bathing at McDonald's and the Pizza by the Slice.

"Go get more," I begged through tears. "Please."

"No, baby. Not tonight."

"Please, Brooks. It's the only way out. Please. Get more."

"Only way out of what?"

"This fucking life," I screeched.

He latched his arm around me tighter. "No. I'm not getting you more E. Not now. You just have to trust me. Trust that I love you. If you believed—"

"Shut up. I know you love me. It doesn't change anything. Get more E."

"No." His voice dripped with hurt. "I'll get us back to what we were. You just have to trust me."

I cried harder and Brooks pressed himself against me until I fell into a restless sleep.

I woke alone and reached for my phone. No text from Brooks. Fear slithered over me. I dialed his latest number, but he didn't pick up. I walked into Gary and Bruce's room, but they mumbled they hadn't seen him and I should go back to sleep.

I paced and called Brooks again.

Finally around noon, almost an hour after Gary and Bruce left for work, when I'd gone from scared to frantic, Brooks came home.

I lashed out the moment he walked into the living room. "Where've you been? Why did you leave me?"

"Baby . . ." He gave me a lazy and too-happy smile. Dread washed over me.

"What are you on?"

He pulled me in to him, his hands touching every bare part of my flesh. "You feel so good. I can't get enough of you. Take off your clothes."

I stepped back. "Did you do more E?"

He grinned.

I held out my hand. "Where's mine?"

"No. Not for you. Not this time. You crash too hard."

I swallowed. "You're doing E without me?"

He pulled open the backpack that he'd dropped on the floor when he walked in. "It's just an appetizer . . ."

"An appetizer for what?"

He lifted up a utility knife. "For this."

I stumbled back. "What? No. Not when you're high."

He reached for me, but I stepped back. Anger lanced through me, warring with fear over what he planned to do with the knife.

"It'll be better when I'm high."

I shook my head. "Everything is better when we're high, right? Do you want to know why? Because it's the only fucking way to make this life livable."

"Aww, Gannon, don't start with that." He raked fingers through his hair, fingers I used to love and crave. "You'll kill my buzz."

"Where's my E?" I demanded, holding a hand out. "I want it to be better too."

"No. No more E for you. I'm not listening to you crash again. I have a better idea." He held up the knife and slid the blade in and out.

"I told you I don't want it."

"It's not for you, baby. I'd never do that to you. Not when I couldn't be sure how it felt."

My body went cold. "What's it for, then?"

He grinned again and walked into our bedroom. I should have left. I knew it; every fiber of my being screamed to get out. But I was too scared.

Brooks dropped on the bed and pulled off his shirt. The

tattoo looked even redder against the paleness of his skin. "You're everything to me," he said, sliding the blade out of the casing and leaving it out this time. "You have to know that."

"I do. What are you doing with the knife?" Fear popped inside me.

Before my mind could wrap itself around what was happening, he cut two angry slashes into his arm. Thin lines of bright red.

"One for the fire. And one for juvie."

"Jesus. Stop." I lunged for him, but he pushed me back, so strong from the E or from whatever point he was trying to make. He wrapped his legs around me and flipped me beneath him. I squirmed and he shifted his knees up, pinning my shoulders.

"You think I wanted this life, Gannon? I gave up everything. I fucking ran into a fire for you. I went to juvie and did horrible things to get back to you. And you fucking buckled at the first sign of trouble. You doubted us. You doubted me."

"Brooks, please. Stop."

He slashed at his arm again, deeper this time. "And this one is so my princess has food and a roof over her head."

"Please. I'm sorry. I'm so sorry."

I reared up, but his legs held firm. Blood poured off his arm onto the bed. He made another slash, deeper. Too much blood.

"Baby, please," I begged. "You don't know what you're doing. You don't feel it. The E—"

"Why did you give up on us?" he screamed. The bed shook, from him or me I couldn't tell. Nothing was registering beyond how much blood was dripping from his arm.

"I didn't give up," I babbled, tears choking my words. "Brooks. Oh God. You're going to hurt yourself. I don't want this."

He ignored me. He barely even looked at his arm, just slashed again and again. I cried and pleaded, but he swung his head back and forth. "I fucking love you. I would do anything for you. I want the pain. Your pain. You don't have to carry it anymore. Give it to me."

And then the knife hit a vein.

He cried out this time as blood gushed from him and his legs gave out. He curled onto his side and dropped the knife.

"Oh God. Oh God. What have you done?" I pressed my hand against his arm. But it was so much blood. It pulsed out of him so fast.

I couldn't see through the tears. Through the blood. I fumbled for my phone and dialed 911.

"What's your emergency?" the operator said.

I didn't even recognize my voice as I said, "Blood—so much blood. I think he's dying. He's bleeding so much."

"Ma'am. You have to calm down. Tell me where you are and what happened."

The words strangled me. I pressed my hand harder against

the slashes on Brooks's arm and he winced. His eyes were shut. I tried to describe the location of our apartment, but all I could spit out was "Across from McDonald's. There's no bathroom. All the blood. Please help him."

His breath changed and I cried out again. The operator continued to talk to me, but I couldn't answer any more questions. Terrified sobs spilled out of me.

The wait was endless, her talking to me, asking me questions, telling me to calm down. Brooks growing paler and paler beside me. And me crying and pleading for them to get there faster.

I pressed harder into his arm, but the blood wouldn't let up. He was so still; I couldn't feel him breathing.

"Brooks. Hang on. Oh God. Baby, hang on. Don't give up on me. Jesus. Oh God."

Covered in blood and suffocating in my own despair, I cried louder. Sirens. Voices. Hands wrapped around me, pulling me away from the abyss, from the spot on the bed where I'd curled in to Brooks. Fingers digging into my shoulders, dragging me back. Screaming. Them. Me. Screaming. For Brooks. For us. Pleading. Screaming. Always screaming.

Begging for help that came too late.

Epilogue

Three months later

"Hand me the wrench," Ricardo said from beneath the sink. My sink. My apartment. My life.

I plucked it out of the toolbox and placed it in his hand. Then went back to staring at the traffic on the street. The parking lot lights at the Punkin' had been flipped on in anticipation of the night crowd. Most of the smokers had left to go hang out at the skate park.

"I think that should do it." Ricardo stood up and wiped his hands across his jeans. Stubby hands. "Now you have a fully functional disposal. Do you want to give it a try?"

I shrugged.

Ricardo shook his head and moved to my refrigerator. "I'll

bet you have some nasty takeout in here that you probably need to get rid of."

"No."

"Well, something else, then." He swung open the fridge door. "Gannon. Why isn't there any food in here?"

I bit my lip. "Haven't gotten around to getting groceries."

A car pulled in to the parking lot of the Punkin'. Honda Civic. My stomach knotted and my hands started to shake. Brooks was everywhere. Even in the stupid little things. I couldn't exorcise him. Even throwing his ashes into the Mississippi hadn't helped. Every minute of every day was an effort to let go of him.

Ricardo saw my hands and turned to search for what had set me off. Nothing. Everything. He moved across the room and grabbed his sweatshirt, pulled it on over his head. Turned back to me.

"I'll take you grocery shopping."

I shook my head. "Not really up for it tonight."

"Maybe you could call your mom and ask her to drop some off."

"No." I couldn't. She called the store every other day, but words never came when Dennis handed me the phone. I listened to her babble about the boys and after a few minutes I hung up.

Ricardo tucked his hands into his jeans pockets. "Well, I was thinking about going to see a movie. Do you wanna come? I'll buy you Junior Mints."

I gave him a half smile. It was all I'd eat out of Dennis's dusty candy box at the store. Ricardo smiled back, so much hope on his face. I hated that he'd spent time investing in me. But he was leaving soon. Which was fine. Everyone left eventually.

"No, thanks."

He released a long breath, scrubbed a hand over his buzz cut.

"When, Gannon?"

The bluntness of his question stirred something inside me. A tiny spark. Probably nothing, maybe. I slid my hands over the scars on my stomach. I could feel them even through the thin fabric of my T-shirt. Or maybe I just thought I felt them.

"Gannon." He snapped his fingers and I dropped my hands. "No more kid gloves with you. When?"

I took a deep breath and the spark flared. Bigger now, not enough to mean much, but still a flare of heat after numbing cold for so long. "I don't know, Ricardo. I honestly don't know."

"Well, I guess that's better than never."

I shrugged again. Even the pull of my shoulders hurt somehow. "It's all I've got."

He stepped in front of me and gave me a hug I didn't return. It was the first time anyone had touched me since I got home. He smelled all wrong. Too clean. Too good. "It's okay, Gannon. It's enough. For now, it's enough."